SURVIVE

AND

ESCAPE

Book One in *The Blue Lives Apocalypse* Series

a novel by

Lee West

Dedication

To the brave men and women in blue—who proudly serve our communities.

And to my family, for their never-ending love and support.

Other Work by Lee West

The Blue Lives Apocalypse Series
Post-Apocalyptic/Dystopian/Action Thrillers

SURVIVE AND ESCAPE (BOOK 1)
RESIST AND EVADE (BOOK 2)
PROTECT AND SERVE (BOOK 3)

The Reckoning Series
Post-Apocalyptic/Action Thrillers

THE MUTINY (BOOK 1)

SURVIVE AND ESCAPE

— 1 —

A wide beam of golden sunlight streamed through the tent screen, warming Jane Archer's tanned face. She shifted in the sleeping bag, taking in the deep aromatic smell of Sam's camp coffee. Stretching lazily in her sleeping bag, Jane called out to Sam.

"Do you have any fresh-baked scones to go with that burnt coffee?"

"I'm afraid the menu is limited to stale muesli and reconstituted powdered milk," said Sam.

"Ugh," she groaned, and then shrugged on her trail-weary khaki shorts and equally grimy T-shirt.

"Hey, I heard that. A little love for the chef would be appreciated."

Coming up behind Sam, Jane wrapped her long toned arms around his neck and nibbled on his ear.

"A little love is all you're looking for?" she whispered in a low sensuous voice.

"Just a little, but I'll take all you're giving." He pulled her onto his lap and nuzzled her closer.

"I can't believe this is our last morning out here. Back to reality."

"Me either. I thought after two weeks I would be more

than ready for a hot shower and real food."

Waving a hand in front of her face, Jane said, "A shower sounds pretty good right now. I don't think the freshwater rinses we've been doing have really done the trick for either of us. Although I have loved skinny-dipping in the mountain streams."

"Me too," he said with a devious smirk. "No rush to get out of here. We're roughly ten miles from the trailhead and our car. We can take our time hiking out. It'll only take half the day to get to the car, plus an hour or so to drive home."

"Sounds like a plan. How do you think Lea has fared?" said Jane before gingerly sipping her coffee without a grimace.

"Lea is a tough kid. People change. She can change back into her pre-*Tank* self," said Sam.

"I hope so. Eight weeks in rehab did her wonders. I just hope we can keep Tank away long enough to give her recovery the time needed to take root."

"With any luck one of your colleagues in the PD will have arrested Mr. Travis for drug trafficking, human trafficking, assault, rape or any number of other felonies I'm sure he's guilty of."

The thought of Tank's previous and potential rap sheet left her feeling pessimistic—and a little queasy.

"Tank has a way of just narrowly escaping our grasp at every turn—but no one can remain lucky forever. We'll catch him involved in something that will stick. Hopefully, Lea will be far away from him when that happens."

"Lea is twenty-four, with the whole world in front of her—and she has amazing parents, if I might say so," said Sam, producing a wide smile.

She nodded hopefully. "I know you're right. I just can't wait to see her."

"Well, let's break camp and start the long hike out of here."

"Sounds good."

As Jane crawled into the tent, she felt Sam's hands on her backside while he moved into the tent with her. With a mischievous glance at Sam, Jane decided their departure could wait a little while longer.

— 2 —

The towering pines stood silent over them, watching as Jane and Sam weaved their way back through the forest to the trailhead and eventually the park entrance. The chattering of birds and insects echoed off the forest walls like voices of a choir in a great cathedral.

Hiking out of the mountains was both a joyous and sad occasion for Jane. Their two-week backcountry trip ended with the usual melancholy that vacation endings always brought. Despite the sadness, the trip's end was also tinged with a degree of triumph. Sam and Jane had more or less passed an important, self-administered test. They'd meticulously planned for the trip, with the intention of thoroughly assessing how they might fare in a real-life emergency situation requiring them to bug out of their neighborhood on foot.

All of the gear and supplies assembled for the two-week backcountry hike had been carefully vetted to sustain them, without resupply, for the duration of the trip. It was a daunting proposition, but when the time came to head out, they couldn't get into the mountains fast enough.

"He'll be fine. The rangers can sort this out," he said. "Plus, we haven't seen anyone in days."

"Okay. Let's speed up. The sooner the rangers get after him, the better."

Back on the trail, they picked up the pace toward the parking lot. Jane frequently glanced over her shoulder as they walked, half expecting to find the distraught man following them, but she never caught a glimpse of him again. As they moved further away from the location of the brief encounter, she relaxed, though she couldn't totally shake the feeling that the man's bizarre appearance in the woods signified a bigger problem.

— 3 —

Sam walked several paces behind Jane, trying his best to keep up. She was moving at double her normal speed, no doubt fueled by their recent run-in on the trail. He began to wonder how long he could keep up the pace. The last time he'd moved this fast for a sustained period was when he was in the field with the Marines, during his time as a Fleet Marine Force corpsman.

"Do you think we can stop to catch our breath? We've been moving at your Bataan Death March pace for more than an hour," he said, struggling to get the words out.

"Sure, I could use a short break."

Sam caught up, putting his hands on his knees and breathing deeply.

"You need to join me a few times a week at the gym for spinning class."

"I'm not riding a stationary bike," he said, still panting.

"Just saying," she added, hands on her hips, scanning the forest around them.

He took a long sip of water from his CamelBak, savoring the pristine taste of filtered mountain-stream water. He wasn't sure how they could go back to drinking the chemically sanitized, chlorine-tinged stuff that poured out of the tap at home. When he'd finally caught his breath, he stood upright, taking in the forest. Something was off.

"We should be close enough for the road traffic to be within earshot. Airport, too."

"I know. It is odd, but there has been no shortage of people passing us," she said.

"Yes. But not the usual assortment of people one might expect in the mountains."

Resting on a rock, Sam glanced down the trail in the direction of their car, wondering what else the day would bring. He couldn't shake the uneasy feeling that something was amiss. Not wanting to alarm Jane, he chose to keep this feeling to himself for now. Jane drank from her CamelBak, catching her breath in between gulps, but he knew her well enough to know she also felt something was off. After twenty-five years of marriage, he considered himself an expert at reading her signals.

"You about ready?" she said.

"Yep, just polishing off the last granola bar."

"I can't even tell you how much I'm looking forward to eating real food."

Sam dusted off his shorts and heaved the burdensome backpack onto his weary shoulders. The weight of his pack seemed to grow the closer they got to the car.

"This looks like a normal bunch," said Jane, nodding toward the trail ahead of them.

A family of four walked in their direction. The parents both carried excessively large packs. The twin children carried packs, which were smaller, but still seemed large for their tiny frames. The mother's head snapped in their direction at the sound of a twig breaking under Jane's foot. The couple seized their children and quickly

9

escorted them off the trail into the dense woods away from Sam and Jane. The family stopped next to a thick tree trunk and huddled together silently, the father standing protectively in front of them. The look on his face told Jane and Sam everything they needed to know. The family was not on vacation.

"Let's pick up the pace," said Jane.

"Good idea."

A little further along the trail, the centuries-old towering trees parted, giving them a view of the parking lot. Cars sat scattered throughout the lot, like large tombstones in an old cemetery. A veil of violence hung over the parking lot, in quiet contrast to the serene surroundings.

"Holy crap," said Sam.

"What the hell?" muttered his wife.

All of the cars in the lot were damaged to some degree. Almost all of the side windows were shattered, the cars' gutted bowels exposed to the elements.

"This is not the work of bears or teenagers," said Jane.

"That's an understatement. No wonder everyone looked pretty freaked out as they passed us. Must have been some sort of massive gang activity or something," said Sam.

"I'm leaning toward the *or something* category," she said. "Our car should be on the south side. I think I see it."

Carefully moving through the devastated lot, Jane and Sam made their way to their car. Sam's Camry had suffered the same fate as the other vehicles. The windshield was smashed, and its side windows were gone, leaving glass beads strewn across the front seats. The trunk had been wrenched open with a crude tool, leaving it open and awkwardly bent.

"Wait a minute. This happened a while ago. Look at the seats. They're covered in wet, decomposed leaves," said Jane.

"Yeah, who knows how long the car has been sitting like this. From the looks of it, I wouldn't be surprised if the vandals were here just after we left, two weeks ago."

Looking at the crushed hood, Jane said, "Do you think it still works?"

"Only one way to find out." Sam dropped his pack to retrieve his car keys.

Carefully opening the door, Sam brushed the glass shards into the driver's foot well. Sam had a sinking feeling that the car wasn't going to start. The key clanged into the key slot with the usual metal-on-metal ting. When he turned the key—nothing. The engine neither groaned nor rumbled to life. It sat completely still, blending seamlessly into the natural environment.

"Do you think the battery is dead?"

"Not sure. It's odd that there was absolutely no sound at all when I turned the key. If the battery was dead, we would have heard the ticking of the relays. But we heard absolutely nothing. I'll pop the hood and see what I can do," said Sam.

Jane dumped her backpack on the ground. "Okay, while you do that, I think I'll have a look around at the other vehicles to try to piece together what happened."

"Sounds good, just stay within earshot."

"Will do."

Sam knew he could fix almost anything. His fellow Marines had dubbed him "MacGyver," a name he openly encouraged. Sam had every tool available for purchase or trade, and a number of custom tools he created by welding various parts together. He loved tinkering in his basement workshop, and over the years people had come to rely on Sam for the odd custom pieces he hand fabricated to solve their mechanical problems.

Opening the hood and peering into the car's guts, he wasn't sure he could make a rapid diagnosis. The engine looked completely untouched. Checking connections, wiring and hoses, he could see no obvious reason for the mechanical failure, leaving him with nothing to fix. Unless he could pinpoint the problem and repair it with the limited tools in his pack, they'd have to walk home. Judging from the parking lot mess, he somehow doubted twenty-four-hour AAA roadside assistance was currently available.

— 4 —

Jane walked slowly through the parking lot, watching for movement between the cars ahead of her. A dozen or so vehicles of various makes and models sat useless in the gravel field, which was bordered by dense forest. Someone clearly liked breaking glass. Random tires had been slashed and most of the trunks were pried open by the same crude hand that had visited their car. Jane had seen enough gang violence and teenage shenanigans to know that either group could have been involved in this crime scene. However, what she saw next unsettled her to the core.

A pickup truck sat still, with its hood open. Nothing seemed amiss in the engine compartment other than the thin layer of leaves and sticks that had accumulated. She moved closer to take a look inside the truck, finding the key pushed snugly into the ignition.

"You find anything?" asked Sam while walking up to her.

"Yes and no. All the cars are damaged. Obviously. But look at this." Jane pointed to the open hood of the pickup truck. "There's a good coating of leaves and

13

sticks, like the hood has been open for a while—and the owner just left the keys in the ignition. Why would anyone do that?"

"The only reason I would leave my keys in the ignition is if it didn't matter." Sam glanced at the vehicle. "If my car had just become a two-ton paperweight, and I knew it."

"Exactly." Jane gazed across the parking lot of disabled cars. "Geez, what happened here?"

"I'm not sure. Walking over to you, I noticed that most of the gas tanks are open. I think someone siphoned out the gas."

"Crap. This is more than some kids messing around drunk on a weekend. We need to get out of here, fast. Do you think you can fix the car?" she asked.

"I'm not sure what's wrong with it. The whole system seems to have died. I brought some very basic tools. I thought that if I could isolate the problem, then I could scavenge parts from the other vehicles to fix ours, " he suggested.

"You don't sound optimistic?"

"I inspected a few of the cars and trucks on the way to meet you. The engines looked fine, but none of them had power."

"How do you know?"

"I tested them by hitting the hazard lights. The ones I tested failed to blink. This isn't to say that all of the cars are disabled."

"I'm calling for a tow truck. I have to let Lea know we'll be delayed," she said.

"I'm not sure we'll get a cell signal out here."

"Sure we will. I called Lea one last time from here before we hiked out."

"That's right. Give it a try. While we're waiting for the tow truck, we can go to the ranger station and report what we saw on the trail."

Rummaging around her backpack, Jane finally got her hands on her cell phone. Her anxiety level eased when the phone powered up. The relief was short lived.

"Darn it. No signal. I called Lea from this exact spot before we took off on the trail. The signal was fine then. In fact, I recall looking at the bars and being amused that we were getting a signal in such a remote area," she said.

"I know this might sound survivalist paranoid, but I have a bad feeling that it's not just the cars or phone that don't work."

"Me too. Everything feels off." Jane rifled through her pack.

"What are you looking for?"

Jane's hands moved quickly and deliberately through her belongings. She pulled out two concealed-carry holsters, handing the black leather holster to Sam and keeping the deep brown rig for herself.

"Do you really think we need these?" said Sam, taking his holster reluctantly.

"Better safe than sorry." Jane removed the Glock 19 from her holster and chambered a round from the already seated magazine. "I suggest you do the same."

She replaced her pistol and lifted the right side of her shirt to slip the holster inside her pants and attach it to the belt holding up her shorts.

"Whatever happened here is old news. Possibly a warm-up for what we may now be facing out there. We need to move fast and be ready to fight our way back to Lea, no matter what it takes," said Jane.

"I'm with you," said Sam, strapping an identical pistol in place on his right hip. "We'll get back to her—one way or another."

"All of it, and knowing when to distract me. We both know that if you weren't here, I would've dropped this pack and started running the twenty miles home to find Lea."

"True. And heaven help anyone in your path," Sam said, caressing her cheek with his strong hand.

Continuing along the path, their moment of levity evaporated when the ranger's station came into view. The door swung lifelessly in the wind. Most of the windows were shattered.

"Not good," she said.

"Looks like the place has been trashed. Abandoned, too. Let's have a look anyway. Maybe something in there will help us piece things together." Sam disappeared into the building.

Jane stood on the threshold of the ranger's cabin, watching him pick through the wreckage inside.

"They dismantled everything. Even the wires to the radios are gone," said Sam.

The shock of their situation and the ramifications for Lea started to settle in on her.

"Lookey, lookey, what we have here. Nice piece of mountain ass," announced a deep male voice, followed immediately by the sound of guys laughing.

Jane spun to face the owner of the voice, catching her pack on the side of the door. She teetered on the granite steps for a brief moment, quickly regaining her balance. When she squared her stance in the doorway, she found herself facing three men in their mid to late twenties—all filthy and covered from top to bottom in scratches and cuts, big and small. They looked ragged, like they had been on the run and exposed to the elements for a long time. They reminded Jane of the escaped prisoners her department had found in town after several days of living in dumpsters, eating trash and drinking from puddles. Except these guys looked worse.

"You get lost from your nice little suburb, lady?" said another one of the men.

"What's in that sweet backpack of yours, baby? I could use a few things," said the first man.

"Looks like you could use some protecting out here. I'll take real good care of you," said the first man, taking a step toward Jane, with a hand on his crotch.

Jane pulled her shirt up and reached for the gun tucked snugly in its holster against her right hip.

"She has a husband who will blow your heads off if you take another step forward," said Sam, suddenly appearing next to her, his pistol aimed straight into the group.

"Damn, look what we have here. It's Hawaii Five-0," said one of the men, eliciting a round of laughter from his friends.

"You ain't got the balls to cap us, hoss. I can tell. Shit, you can't even hold your gun steady," said another man, a bold look on his grimy face.

In her peripheral vision, she could tell her husband's grip was shaky, which these punks mistakenly interpreted as weakness. Adrenaline, maybe, but not the kind of fear they assumed. Jane had no doubt her husband could and would drop all of them if necessary. She needed to defuse this situation before it reached that boiling point.

"If he doesn't, then I sure as hell do," said Jane, drawing her pistol and aiming it at the leader's head. "Evansville PD. Stop where you are and put your hands where I can see them."

"Peeee...Deeee? You a dying breed, police lady," said

one of the men, laughing.

This group was unbelievably brazen, especially with weapons aimed at them. For a moment, she wasn't sure this would end peacefully.

"Come on, guys, a piece of old ass ain't worth it," said the leader. "You better watch your back, bitch. You ain't got no backup anymore."

The men nonchalantly walked back to the trail, sneering at them and laughing until they were out of sight.

"Old ass? Really? I should have blasted them for that comment alone," said Jane as she holstered her Glock.

"Maybe we should keep these out just in case," said Sam, visibly shaken by the exchange.

"No, my guess is that they're gone, and they have no intention of following us. Guys like that focus on the low-hanging fruit. They had no weapons and rightfully assessed that they were outgunned in this battle," said Jane.

"I guess. What do you suppose he meant by the police being a dying breed?"

"I'm not sure, but I didn't like the sound of it."

"Neither did I. Maybe we'll see someone normal on the trail. Someone we can talk to without a confrontation."

"I don't know. Given the people we've run into thus far, I think we need to get off the trail entirely and avoid everyone unless we can somehow assess they're not a threat," she said.

"Good point. Let's look at the map and think about where to go from here." Sam pulled a folded map from one of his cargo pockets. "Watch the door for us."

Sam spread the worn map across the counter in the

ranger's station and started tracing his finger across the trails while Jane positioned herself where she could see both the map and the door.

"We're here. So…if we take this trail north, we could ditch the trail at this point and cut through the forest to this ridge. We'd be heading in the general direction of Evansville, in a good position to exit the park tomorrow morning," said Sam.

"Tomorrow morning? You want to stay here tonight? I think we need to keep going. Who knows what's happening with Lea. I don't want to waste any more time. She could be in real danger."

"I know. But at a normal pace, we're looking at a two-day hike to our house. Minimum. Two long days, taking the quickest route, and we really don't know if that route will be clear. Besides, it's almost five. We only have a few more hours of daylight."

She nodded, muttering a curse under her breath. "All right. Do you remember Charlie from the PD? You met him about a year ago at Sid's retirement party. He lives in Porter. It's roughly halfway between here and Evansville, pretty much in our path. I think we should head out before first light tomorrow and get to his house as fast as we can. He lives by himself in a fairly remote location. The guys always rib him about living like a hermit. We can figure out what's happening and rest there before setting off on the second half of the hike."

"Sounds like a plan. Let's get out of here before more *hikers* pass through. This is probably ground zero for anyone in the area looking for help, and the last place we should be."

Sam refolded the map with shaky hands, placing it back in his pocket.

Jane gripped his hand. "Hey, it will be okay. We'll get home."

"I'm not worried about that. It made me crazy to see those men acting like that toward you. What they wanted to do," he said.

"All in a day's work. Those guys were relatively harmless. Just looking to score whatever they could. I could tell they weren't the hardened types who will kill a person for no reason at all." She squeezed his hand tighter.

"I know you're in danger every day, but seeing you in danger up close really rattled me."

Wrapping her arms around his waist, Jane hugged Sam tightly. "You did great back there. I could barely tell you aren't a pro."

He forced a laugh. "Yeah, right. My gun was shaking so badly, I thought I would shoot you in the process of pulling off my knight-in-shining-armor routine."

Pushing back from Sam, but keeping hold of his hands, Jane smiled. "You have been and will always be my knight in shining armor. But maybe you should leave the gun flashing to me."

"Deal. You ready to get going?"

"Ready as ever."

— 6 —

They hiked for almost an hour through the woods, mostly off the trail. For the short time they followed the trail, if they heard someone coming, they quickly sought cover in the trees and scrub until the hikers moved on. Sam now understood why the family they'd seen earlier in the day chose to scurry off the trail and hide from them. The family knew, as they did now, that the biggest threat to their safety came from the other humans. He finally found a tucked-away place to spend the night on the ridge they had identified on the map. The location was deep in the forest, off the beaten path and far from prying eyes. It also gave them a commanding view of the valley below.

"Do you think a fire is a good idea?" asked Jane.

"As much as I would like to say yes, I don't think it is. Do you?"

"Not really, but I was hoping you would talk me into lighting one. I could go for some hot food."

"Reconstituted chum isn't cutting it for you anymore?"

"Frankly, I'd rather go hungry than eat another one of your survival meals. What time do you want to get moving tomorrow?" She opened a zipped bag of granola.

24

"The sun rises around 6:30 a.m. We should have enough light to make our way up and out around 5:30. If everything goes as planned, we should be at Charlie's house around dinnertime or at least before it gets too dark again to navigate."

Jane exhaled while quietly staring at the ground. Sam knew something was wrong. Jane was not a quiet person unless she was either upset or sick.

"How are you doing?"

"Worried. What do you think is happening with Lea? It's beyond frustrating to be this far away, unable to check in with her."

"I know. We'll see her soon enough. At the very least, we'll get a handle on what's happening from Charlie. That will help us a lot. My guess, given the condition of the cars in the lot, is that an EMP caused the damage."

"I was hoping you wouldn't say that. I wonder what caused it and how far the damage spreads?"

"If it is an EMP, the area affected could be widespread, as in half of the country. The cause? We may never know. And it probably doesn't matter. All we can do is focus on keeping ourselves safe until things get back to normal," he said, adding, "If they ever get back to what passed as normal."

"I have a really bad feeling we may never see normal again," she said before yawning deeply.

"Come on, we should get some sleep, or at least try to. We have two long days ahead of us." He took her hand and helped her up.

Inside their two-person tent, Sam and Jane lay entwined in each other's arms. Sam never tired of the moments he spent holding her. In her arms he felt both invincible and helpless. He loved her with the same intensity now as ever. Breathing in the sweet smell of her hair, he lightly kissed her head before drifting off.

~ ~ ~

Jane lay there, recently woken from a light sleep. *Darn it. I have to pee.* She hated the complications of going to the bathroom in the woods, especially in the middle of the night. Prior to retiring for the evening, Jane always made a mental map of the site and a plan for later, when she would inevitably have to get up to relieve herself. Tonight was no different. She knew she needed to circle behind the tent in order to stay clear of the ridgeline and its obvious dangers. Trying not to wake Sam, Jane slowly and carefully unzipped the tent and made her way into the steamy night air.

Standing up straight, she stretched her back and yawned. As she pivoted to head behind the tent, she froze. Shaking the sleepy haze, she stared over the ridge into the valley. *That can't be right.*

"Sam, Sam, wake up. You have to see this," she hissed. She stuck her foot into the tent and nudged Sam's leg. "Come on, wake up."

"What is it? Are you hurt?" said Sam, rustling to get out of his sleeping bag.

"No, just get up. I need to show you something."

Sam slowly got up and joined her near the ridgeline. Standing side by side, holding hands, Sam and Jane looked in the direction of the valley—seeing a vast darkness. The sounds of the forest intensified, enveloping them in fear. The sheer expanse of the blackness was unlike anything either of them had ever seen. No lights twinkled in the distance. Not a single illuminated road snaked through the landscape. A changed world lay before them, requiring nothing short of raw survival.

— 7 —

The hike out of the park was mercifully uneventful. They managed to avoid most people on the trail by either sneaking off into a concealed location as other hikers walked past, or staying off the trail entirely. The few people they did encounter seemed to be harmless, lost souls, looking for refuge in the park. Despite their string of good fortune avoiding a confrontation throughout the day, Sam worried that their luck would run out. He knew the contents of their packs were worth more than gold in this changed world. The supplies they carried on their backs allowed them to survive without support for at least a few more days, depending on how much they ate. Such an open display of resources made them targets for those less fortunate.

"Do you recall exactly where Charlie's house is?" asked Sam, his voice weary.

"Not really. I know it's just past Porter, going toward Evansville. I think once we get into town, I should be able to recognize the street."

"I don't think it's a good idea for us to walk through town." Sam shifted the weight of his pack.

"I've been thinking the same thing, but going through

Porter will allow us to get a handle on the situation. We don't even know when all of this started, whatever all of this is."

"Okay. Porter is a small town. We stay off Main Street and we should be fine. Let's look at the map for a minute to figure out the best way in." Sam produced a new map from one of his cargo pockets.

"I didn't know you brought a state map? I figured we would be moving with just a compass after leaving the park."

"Really? What kind of survivalist would I be if I didn't carry an area map?" said Sam before winking.

Spreading the map on the ground, Jane easily pointed out the location of Charlie's road. Sam knew she could do it with a map in front of her. He was relieved that he'd decided to include the state map—a last minute addition he'd almost left at home.

"If we take Liberty most of the way, we should be able to leapfrog behind buildings, mostly keeping off the main roads. Then we can cut across this farm and approach Charlie's from the west," she said, tracing the map with a stick.

"Based on the pace we maintained, we might not get to Charlie's house before seven tonight."

"Probably not. Why do you look so worried?"

"Well, if we get delayed in any way, we might end up at his house after dark. We have no way to let him know we're coming, and I would prefer not to get shot."

"Good point. The only way to guarantee a daylight arrival is to pick up the pace. What do you think about ditching some of our stuff to lighten the load? Maybe if we can move faster, we'll avoid trouble on the road. Moving faster and avoiding trouble might be more useful than some of the things in our packs. Besides, we have everything we need at home to survive for a long time."

"I would love a break from this pack, and being more nimble, especially in a populated area, isn't a bad idea. But we have no idea what we're facing or how long we might be on our own. This is especially true if an EMP caused the electrical outage. We also don't know what we'll find at home. Our supplies might not be there when we get back. I think we both know that," said Sam, in a kind voice.

"I know. It has been easier for me to visualize Lea waiting for us in a house stocked to the gills than face any other scenario."

"Let's try to pick up the pace as much as possible. We have to deal with one thing at a time right now."

They walked hand in hand toward the town of Porter.

— 8 —

Porter stood quietly in front of them, beckoning Jane and Sam to step out of the forest. Maybe a little too quiet. Following the plan, Sam and Jane moved quickly along Liberty Road, catching glimpses of Main Street as they made their way through the outer edge of town. Porter's once lively and quaint downtown area had been ransacked. Most of Main Street's ground-floor windows had been broken; the doors were either ripped off the hinges or sitting wide open with no sign of resistance. The sheer desolation rattled Jane.

"Where is everyone?" asked Jane.

"That's the big question. You'd think we'd see or hear some kind of activity. Unless—"

"I know what you were going to say," she said. "Hold on. I want to check something out. Wait here."

"What? What do you mean wait here? Where are you going?" He leaned up against the remains of a smashed car.

"I just want to get a clearer view up Main Street. I keep having this unshakable feeling that we're being watched. I'll be right over there—no big deal. I'll stay concealed."

Jane dropped her pack next to Sam and quickly jogged between the buildings to the corner. She slowly peered around the side of the building, scanning Main Street. What she found deeply disturbed her.

Bullet holes riddled the buildings in frantic crisscross patterns. The holes indicated that the shots were fired from both directions, into the buildings and from the buildings themselves. Massive dark stains adorned the sides of the buildings and human remains littered the walkways. Crudely written graffiti covered some of the structures, taking her breath away.

DOWN WITH PIGS—KILL THEM ALL!

Many simply stated *NEW ORDER*. A few appeared to have been scripted in blood. The darkened substance streamed down from the crude letters in a macabre reminder of just how far things had changed. Jane had no doubt this was a warning to those threatening the "new order." Either way she knew they needed to get away from here as fast as possible.

Turning to return to Sam, Jane froze in her tracks at the sound of a large engine rumbling down the street. Out in the open, with only the side of the building to shield her, Jane knew she needed to make a quick decision. Run to Sam or find concealment nearby. Sensing she wouldn't have time to reach Sam, she dove behind a large metal dumpster next to the building, hoping she would not be seen from the street. She glanced at Sam to be sure he heard the vehicle's approach.

Sam peered at her from around the side of the derelict vehicle, where he had rested during her scouting mission. His face mirrored the sheer panic she felt. Jane knew she could not move to him until the threat passed. She signaled to him to stay put and that something was coming. He nodded and quickly heaved their packs into the back of the car to keep them hidden from view.

A dusty old red pickup truck moved slowly down Main Street, headed in her direction. Jane willed herself to melt into the brick façade of the building she leaned against, certain that the vehicle's arrival signaled trouble. Her instinct paid off.

Five rough and hardened-looking men, wearing face-shielding bandanas, rode in the back of the pickup truck; the words NEW ORDER were spray-painted in white on the side facing Jane. Each carried a different weapon. A few had pump-action shotguns similar to those fielded by local police departments. The rest carried crude, makeshift weapons like shovels, hammers and pitchforks.

Tied to the rear bumper of the truck, a naked man walked shackled and handcuffed. The man's face was badly beaten—his eyes swollen shut. He blindly shuffled forward, a garland of golden police shields clinking around his neck. Jane recoiled in horror when she saw the man's various bruises and the deep angry red lash marks crossing his back.

"Make him run!" yelled one of the men.

The shouts and laughter of the other men rang out in the once peaceful town. The driver sped up, causing the man to pick up his pace to a fast jog.

"Run, pig!" shouted another man.

Eventually the chained man stumbled and fell, his body leaving a bright red streak down the center of the road as it dragged behind the truck. She lost sight of the macabre spectacle as the truck sped away, not daring to move her head to readjust her view. Judging by the squealing of tires as the truck rounded a corner down the street, she couldn't imagine the man tied to the back had survived.

It took Jane a few minutes to recover from what she'd just witnessed. She looked at Sam and wondered if he'd seen the same thing. Given the look on his face, she assumed he'd witnessed enough. Jane jogged over to Sam as fast as she could.

"Did you see that?" she asked desperately.

"I wish I hadn't. Can't un-see something like that. What is going on?"

"I have no idea. He had a string of police shields around his neck. My guess is that he was Porter PD. We need to get off the streets, fast."

Rifle shots pierced the quiet town, causing them to question where they could find safety in the New Order.

— 9 —

Rusty Evans sat in her rocking chair, slowly swaying to remembered music playing in her head. The sound of rifle fire touched her ears, but roused no reaction. Gunfire, shouts and the tortured screams of neighbors were the new norm for Porter residents. She did the best she could to stay clear of the shuttered windows, just like her grandson, Johnny, had advised.

"Ain't nothing good to see, Granny," was what he'd said before being forced to leave by the men claiming to be the new police.

She hoped Johnny would talk sense into the men. Convince them to stop the horrible things they were doing. Mostly she hoped Johnny would come home in one piece. Things had fallen apart since the lights went out. She had two cans of string beans left in her pantry, and the water had stopped running a few days ago. She'd filled the tub, sinks and all of her pots, pans and glasses with water, like her Johnny had told her—but the supply wouldn't last forever.

The muted thump of a car door quietly closing drew her attention. Sounds like that got the better of her curiosity. Someone was sneaking around. Maybe her grandson was back. Instead of Johnny, she saw a man and woman hiding behind her neighbor's smashed car. Although she did not recognize them, she did recognize the look. They were runners. People either trying to get out of town or passing through in a hurry. In either case, things generally did not end well for that sort of folk.

Looking a little further past the couple, Rusty spotted a red streak running down Main Street and turning onto Ash Street. A bloodied body punctuated the end of the grisly line, lying crumpled against a telephone pole beyond the intersection. Looking closely, Rusty was able to identify the body as that of Deputy Robert Seits of the Porter Police Department.

Like the others, he was a nice man who had always done a good job for the people of Porter. She wondered how many police officers were left. Looking at Deputy Seits's necklace, she knew there could not be many. The first officer killed wore one badge. Each officer after the first added his or her own badge to the necklace.

Going back to her rocking chair, Rusty sat down wearily, knowing she would have to wait a little longer for Johnny to return. If anyone could keep her safe, it was her grandson. He'd survived far longer than most his age.

— 10 —

Strings of burs from the field they crossed covered Sam's pants pricking against his exposed hands when they brushed against his legs. Normally, he'd spend the time removing each and every annoying bur, but they were on a tight timeline to reach Charlie's house before dark. Sam estimated that Charlie's house sat a quarter mile into the woods beyond the field. Their progress had been slow. Each time a *New Order* truck with its mean-looking men rumbled past, they were forced to seek a concealed location.

At one point, Sam was sure they had been spotted by one of the men. An extremely tall, lanky New Order guard looked right at Sam before casually turning away. He would have sworn the two of them locked eyes. If Sam had to guess, he would say the man chose to ignore them. He wasn't about to stake his and Jane's lives on that guess, but it gave him some hope that the world hadn't completely gone insane. After the encounter, they moved slowly and carefully, each movement thought out to maximize their stealth.

Several yards beyond the tree line, Sam halted. "Let's take a break. I need to make a last minute adjustment to our trek."

"Okay. I have to pee anyway," replied Jane.

Placing their packs on the ground, Sam and Jane sat facing each other.

"I cannot believe that we saw three New Order trucks and no other vehicles," said Jane.

"It's almost like any working vehicle has been commandeered for their use. They look like lunatics."

"I wonder what else has been commandeered for their use," she said, a disgusted look on her face. "I'll be right back. Just a quick trip to the ladies' room."

Sam watched Jane walk along the tree line. He knew she needed privacy, but hated having her out of his sight. Considering the circumstances, he wished she would relieve herself a little closer. Instead, to his complete annoyance, she insisted on walking a good distance from him and disappearing into the woods. *Women*, Sam thought as he gulped warm water from his dirty CamelBak hose.

"Flat on the ground, asshole," said the deep voice of a hidden man.

A furtive glance over his shoulder revealed a man wearing military-style woodland camouflage. A matching body-armor vest, several bulging magazine pouches, and a suppressed AR-15-style rifle told Sam he was either saved or screwed. The suppressor worried him. This guy could shoot them and nobody would hear it.

"Okay, you got—"

"No talking. Slowly lower yourself to the dirt or I blast a hole through your miserable head," said the man in a loud whisper.

Sam lay flat on the ground, his nose pressed against the dirt and his sweaty fingers laced behind his head. Thoughts of Jane consumed him. Unsure of her location or if the man acted alone, Sam sought to buy time. He hoped Jane would see the interaction and remain hidden.

"I'm just walking through town. I'm not causing harm to anyone," said Sam in a loud voice.

He hoped to alert Jane before she returned so that she would remain hidden until he could handle the situation.

"I don't give a shit where you think you and your friend are going, you're not going there now. Slide your weapon to me, very slowly and very carefully," said the man.

"I'm alone. It's just me," shouted Sam with a scared lilt.

"You always carry two packs, asshole?" said the man.

Sam knew he had only a moment to change his predicament before the man either blew his head off or Jane walked into an ambush. He desperately sought a solution through the dense mental fog of his fear.

"Stand down, Charlie! It's Officer Archer, Evansville PD!" yelled Jane.

Oh shit, here she comes. She should have stayed hidden, thought Sam.

"What the hell?" replied the man.

"Charlie, it's me, Jane Archer. You have my husband on the ground. Please lower your rifle and let him up," pleaded Jane as she cautiously moved toward Charlie.

Jane moved toward the man, carefully positioning herself between Sam and the shooter. Sam twisted his head to get a better look.

"Jane?" said the man, looking at her with stunned recognition. "Geez. Sorry, man. I thought you were another scumbag with the idea to replenish his supplies from my house."

"No worries. Just glad you didn't shoot first and ask questions later," said Sam, trying to force a smile through the anxiety he still felt.

"I usually do, but I saw two packs. Didn't want to start shooting until I could see both of you," said Charlie.

A vehicle engine revved in the distance. Jane and Charlie looked in the direction of the sound.

"Shit. Not them again. Grab your stuff. We have to move fast," said Charlie, with a quick glance around.

Sam jogged behind Jane and Charlie, unsure where Charlie was headed. By his calculations, they should have been going in the opposite direction Charlie ran. After everything they'd witnessed, Sam did not trust anyone, even Charlie. Sensing danger, Sam halted.

"No. We're not going any further until you tell us where we're going," shouted Sam with a rough hand on Jane's shoulder, stopping her.

"Sam, what are you doing?" asked Jane.

"He's taking us in the opposite direction of where you thought we should go. We should be headed in that direction," said Sam, pointing away from the group.

Glancing at Jane, Charlie said, "Suit yourself. But if they catch you, they'll kill you on the spot."

"Okay, guys. Take a deep breath. Sam, could you pull out the map? Perhaps Charlie could show us the location of his house," suggested Jane.

"We don't have time for this," said Charlie.

"Humor me, please," said Jane.

Sam yanked the map out of his pocket and tossed it to Charlie, with an annoyed flick. Charlie unfolded the map, turned it to face them and explained.

"My house is right here," he said, and jabbed his finger on the map.

Sam noted that the place Charlie pointed to was exactly where Jane thought he lived. Sam and Jane looked at each other, stunned.

"Charlie, what is our current location?" asked Jane.

"Right here."

Charlie pointed to a spot nowhere near the location Sam would have guessed they were. Every time they had to hide from a passing vehicle, they must have meandered a little off track. Sam thought they had stayed close enough to the intended route, but judging location became difficult in a wide-open field. Obviously they were way off course.

"You were about to walk straight into the New Order clubhouse. Should've let you volunteer yourself," said Charlie, glancing at Sam.

Realizing their mistake, Sam's face colored a deep red.

"Sorry, man. It has been an unbelievable couple of days. Trust is running thin at this point," said Sam, offering his hand. "Jane speaks very highly of you. I should have taken that as gospel."

Shaking Sam's hand, Charlie said, "As much as I would like to stand around and hug it out, we better get moving."

— 11 —

Sweat rolled down the back of Charlie's neck, soaking the collar of his shirt. Since the water stopped running, Charlie had grown accustomed to being sweaty and dirty most of the time. Showers were a luxury of the past, along with everything else. His home's proximity to a creek put him in a little better position than most, but he hadn't been able to take advantage of it yet. He'd been too busy since the electricity failed—and the chaos descended. Finding Jane and Sam in the woods lifted Charlie's mood. Anxious to hear where they'd been for the past two weeks, Charlie picked up the pace to his home.

After rounding a rustic-looking rock wall on the edge of his property, the old house came into view.

"It's not much, but I like it. You're welcome to stay as long as you need," he said.

"Thanks, Charlie. We plan to be out of your hair before first light," said Sam.

"Why the rush? Looks like the two of you could use a solid frame over your heads for a little while," quizzed Charlie.

"Our daughter, Lea, is alone at the house. We need to

get to her as soon as possible," said Sam, placing his pack on the ground near the door.

"We need to move your packs into a crawl space under the stairs just in case we get unwelcome visitors. I don't want them knowing you're here," said Charlie.

"Who are you talking about? Those New Order thugs?" said Jane before dropping into a chair at Charlie's kitchen table.

"Can I offer you some warm soda? It's all I have left besides the warm water I collected in the tub," said Charlie.

"Single-guy tub water?" said Jane with a raised eyebrow. "I'll take the soda."

They all laughed for a moment.

"Wait, what? How long has the power and water been out? Do you know what happened?" asked Sam, sitting next to Jane.

"Here's all I know. The power went out just after you signed off the duty roster for vacation, Jane. We all figured you were hiding somewhere local, but by the looks of you two, it seems that may have been an incorrect assumption," said Charlie.

"No, we've been hiking in the mountains. We were on an extended backcountry trip. When we came back to our car, we found it vandalized and dead," said Jane. "So what's up with this New Order group?"

"Sounds like you missed all the action. Almost immediately after the lights went out, the inmates at the PrisCorp facility escaped en masse. All eight hundred of them, give or take the few killed during the escape," said Charlie in a grave tone.

"Holy shit," said Jane in a solemn voice.

"What is PrisCorp?" asked Sam.

"PrisCorp is one of those private, for-profit prisons. The state had one in Grant, about ten miles or so from here," said Jane.

"It houses some of the nastiest characters we have. Murderers, rapists and lots of competing gangs," said Charlie.

"The problem is that PrisCorp, like most of the privately run facilities, operates on a shoestring budget. They are woefully understaffed, offering the inmates no sort of distractions, like well-equipped workout facilities and educational opportunities," said Jane.

"Who cares? These are criminals, not guests at a country club. Why entertain them?" asked Sam.

"I'm with you, but all of those things keep them busy, slowing down the gang activity. Without the distractions, the inmates grow very bored and very dangerous. This combination can prove lethal when housing hardened criminals long term," said Charlie. "New gangs, on top of the established gangs, jockey for position within the prison hierarchy."

"Did you say all the inmates are out?" asked Jane.

"Yep. PrisCorp didn't properly maintain their redundant power source as required by the state. What are the chances of an extended power loss, right? They must have figured the generators were enough. They weren't. As soon as the generators lost juice, the doors opened," said Charlie.

"What happened to the guards working there? Or do I not want to ask?" said Jane.

"We think most of them are fine. No bodies were found, so our best guess is that they knew what would happen when the generators ran dry and beat feet before that happened," said Charlie.

"That was probably the right call," said Sam.

"Yeah, great for them, but not for the rest of us. It would have been nice to have a little advance warning. PrisCorp's little mistake dumped eight hundred convicted felons into the community," said Charlie.

"None of the area police departments were notified?" asked Jane.

"Not one. The inmates streamed out of PrisCorp and into Porter first. Now they're active in Evansville. We're not entirely sure, but we suspect two gangs have risen in the aftermath, possibly cooperating—for now," said Charlie.

"We need to get out of here and back to Lea. God only knows what's happening over there. It doesn't sound like she's safe at all," said Jane.

"You can't rush into this without backup or a plan. Trust me. You should head over to CPHQ and see what they can do to help," said Charlie.

"I don't think we have time for that," said Sam. "What is the CPHQ?"

"Clark Provisional Headquarters. The towns of Clark, Porter and Evansville have pooled their remaining resources and created a new, combined police department to get us all through what is happening. We are actively escorting fellow officers to the CPHQ through a chain of friendlies—some fellow cops, military veterans and other regular citizens," said Charlie. "Kind of like an underground railroad."

Shifting uncomfortably in his seat, Sam asked, "What do you mean to *get us through what is happening?*"

"The PrisCorp gangs have taken over Porter and most of Evansville. They're actively hunting down cops and killing anyone in their way. They busted into each town's headquarters and stole the rosters of police. They're also killing military veterans. Anyone they deem capable of mounting a resistance. In some areas they're going house to house, searching for anything or anyone related to the military. Pictures. Plaques. Shadowboxes. Any of it can get you killed. Seems like they think we'll just go down quietly," said Charlie.

"Shit. They know where we live. Lea is there alone. We have to go, now," said Jane, launching up from her chair again.

"No. They don't have the Evansville rosters. When all the shit started hitting the fan, Chief Carlisle had us destroy all the paper records and remove all of the weapons and tactical gear. He even had us go to the evidence locker and remove everything from there, including the chain of custody receipts, since those ID the officer involved," said Charlie.

"Take a seat, Jane. We really can't leave immediately. Charlie is right. We need a plan," said Sam.

"You said there was no warning. How did the chief know to destroy everything?" asked Jane.

"A very brave young man by the name of Johnny Evans tipped me off. He's a local guy, a friend I used to fish with. He was forcibly 'recruited' to the New Order patrols. He risked his life to alert me to lie low and not venture out because most of the Porter PD had been murdered or were being hunted," said Charlie.

"Geez, this is insane," said Jane with a stricken look on her face. "Is it safe to be here?"

"So far so good." Charlie smiled. "But I don't plan to be around for long. We have three more officers that need an escort out of here before I can go to CPHQ. I was waiting for Officer Seits this afternoon. He was supposed to meet me in the woods when I stumbled on the two of you," said Charlie, waving his hand at them wearily.

Sam and Jane glanced at each other uncomfortably.

"I don't think he would've made it. We saw a man paraded through town with a string of police badges around his neck. They killed him," said Sam.

"Shit. Not another one," said Charlie sadly.

The dark circles under his eyes betrayed the deep exhaustion and stress he felt.

"I can't believe that the combined efforts of our three departments aren't enough to fight back these assholes," said Jane in an exasperated voice.

"I guess it might be if we could coordinate our efforts. But with the electrical grid down, we haven't been able to compare notes, let alone coordinate a pushback of the magnitude we need," said Charlie.

"With everything else happening, I forgot about the power. What happened?" asked Sam.

"We're not one hundred percent sure, but most suspect an EMP," said Charlie.

"How widespread is it?" asked Jane.

"Again, we're not really sure, but most think it's the entire Eastern Seaboard at the very least," said Charlie as he opened a can of beans. "Dinner, anyone?"

— 12 —

Sam stood at the guest bedroom window, watching Jane walk slowly down to the creek. She wanted to wash and be alone. They were both shaken by what they'd seen on top of being worried out of their minds for the safety of their daughter. He wondered if Lea was still in the house or if she had been forced to flee to a safer location. By tomorrow evening they should be reunited if all went well. Getting through the next twenty-four hours would be challenging for him. Time stretched to an excruciatingly long period for Sam while he worried for their safety.

Looking around the guest room, Charlie's bachelorhood was evident. The smallish room contained nothing but an old desk and an even older plaid couch. The couch folded out into an uncomfortable sleeper bed. It was lumpy and worn, but an improvement over the ground. Hearing noise from inside the house, Sam decided to see if Charlie needed any help.

"Charlie?" said Sam, peeking down the basement stairs.

"I'm here. Come on down. Just be careful on the stairs. It gets a little tricky at the bottom," said Charlie from the dark basement.

Sam moved slowly down the stairs. He hung on to the rail as best he could, measuring each step of his descent.

"Shit!" yelled Sam as his foot slipped, causing him to stumble down the last step.

"Told ya." Charlie chuckled.

"Geez, you could have told me the last step was the width of a ruler," said Sam.

"Now where's the fun in that?" Charlie smiled.

Sam surveyed the small dimly lit room. Charlie sat at a desk made of roughhewn plywood over cinder block. In front of him sat a rudimentary communications setup consisting of a HAM radio, a few police-grade walkie-talkie sets sitting uselessly in their dead chargers, an expensive-looking handheld CB radio, and a recent model satellite phone. The room was alight from the soft glow of a single candle. On one of the shelves lining the walls, he noticed a few items that looked seriously out of place mixed among the canned foods. Two sets of the latest generation night-vision goggles and several olive drab canister grenades stood out the most.

"Wow, where did you get all of this?" asked Sam.

"Well, the HAM radio is mine, the rest belongs to the Evansville PD. The chief figured since I don't live in Evansville, some of our gear would be safe here, especially since I'm the primary point of contact along the Porter escape route."

"Not a bad call, from what I can tell." Sam asked, "Are those smoke grenades?"

"Smoke and tear gas," said Charlie. "I'm not sure what to do with those."

"I'm sure you'll think of something."

"You'll find this interesting. I just got a message from

Johnny, my contact in the New Order. It seems he saw you and Jane today making a run in this direction. He's not sure anyone else saw you, but we can't take any chances."

"I thought one of their guys looked at me. Is he a tall, lanky, skinny-looking young guy?" asked Sam.

"Yep. That's him. After they 'recruited' him, he has been giving me updates and trying to get the cops and vets out of Porter. He's a very brave man. Without his help, I'm not sure where we would be right now."

"This is all crazy," said Sam, shaking his head.

"Tell me about it," said Charlie, turning and nodding toward a generator on the other side of the small space.

"I was wondering about that."

"I've powered the radio with the generator since the batteries ran dry. I moved it to the basement in order to reduce the sound, then hooked up a pipe to the exhaust and directed that out the window," said Charlie, pointing to the small window.

"How much gas do you have left for the generator?"

"Not much. I took out what I could from my car. I also used the little extra I had around for emergencies and the riding mower. I guess I really didn't plan for this long of an emergency. Who does?"

"Does your car work?" asked Sam.

"Nope. Why?"

"I think I can take the battery from your car and rework the wires from your radio to plug into the car battery. It's worth a try," said Sam. "I'd need a power inverter."

"I have an old cigarette lighter inverter I used to charge my phone in the truck on camping trips, back in the day."

"I can work with that," said Sam. "It won't be pretty or the most efficient, but it'll work."

"That would be amazing. If you can charge up these dead walkie-talkies too, I'll give them to you guys to take with you back to Evansville," said Charlie.

"Sounds like a plan," said Sam, turning to the stairs.

"Careful on the bottom step," said Charlie with a wink.

— 13 —

The cool creek water swirled around Jane's ankles. Slowly, her feet started to feel a little better after their long hike to Charlie's house. Her hiking boots were great for mountain trails, but city walking felt a little like driving with snow tires—too clunky and heavy for the conditions. She crouched low and dipped the top of her head in the water, washing away a few layers of grime. She wished washing away her anxiety was just as easy.

Thoughts of Lea consumed her. To make matters worse, just as soon as she started to focus on her daughter, thoughts of the targeted officers and area veterans made her feel guilty. *Are they really hunting down the cops and vets?*

A low rumbling sound brought her attention back to the moment. Glancing at the house, she could see someone in the garage with a flashlight. After enjoying one last splash of the refreshing water, Jane moved quickly under the light of the moon to the house.

~ ~ ~

"There. That should do it. Give it a try now," said Sam,

nodding at Charlie.

The handheld CB radio crackled to life on the charger, a message coming through.

"Can I pick it up?" said Charlie.

"It's been charging for a few minutes. It should be good for a quick conversation."

"Charlie, Charlie, this is Marta. Over. You there, Charlie? Over," said an unknown voice.

He grabbed the radio. "This is Charlie. Over."

"Hey, Charlie. We're ready here. What's your status? Over," said the woman.

"Yeah, I'm ready to receive. Same place and time? Over," said Charlie.

"Same place and time. Sorry about Deputy Seits. He was a good man. Over," said the woman, risking identification.

"Yeah, me too. Over and out," said Charlie, putting the handset back on the charger.

"Looks like the two of you will have some company if all goes well," said Charlie, turning to Jane and Sam.

"Do you know who it is?" asked Jane.

"No. We're trying to speak as little as possible since we aren't sure who's listening. Marta worked in the administrative division of the Porter PD and has been instrumental in coordinating the escape of their police officers. She's somewhat of a lifesaver. Without her help, not as many officers and vets would have been moved out of harm's way," said Charlie, rubbing his tired eyes. "Tomorrow we'll grab the next runner near where I found the two of you. He or she can go with you to the next safe house."

"Sounds like a plan. When do we leave?" asked Sam.

"Five thirty, just before it starts getting light out. I'll

bring a pack with extra provisions for our guest and get you guys on your way as quickly as possible," said Charlie.

"Where is the next safe house?" asked Jane.

"It's a farm near the border of Grant, just off an old horse trail. The locals still use it when walking in the backcountry. So far there are no reports of New Order activity on the trail. It's pretty deep in the woods, away from the main roads, but runs roughly parallel to Parker Road. Most of PrisCorp's guests would have no idea the trail exists, which is why we're using it," said Charlie.

"That should put us in a spot where we can easily head west to our house, if I'm following you," said Sam, pulling out his map.

"This is about where the trail is and here is Doris Venture's house, the next safe house in the chain," said Charlie, pointing on the well-worn map.

"Okay, that works," said Jane.

"Just make sure to lie low at Doris's house if need be. Things are very dangerous and extremely volatile. We never really know what's happening, and these guys seem to be one step ahead of us all the time," advised Charlie.

"All right, we better get what rest we can before shoving off in a few hours," said Sam, tugging on Jane's arm.

"Hey, thanks for everything, Charlie. You're really doing a lot to save the lives of fellow cops and vets, not to mention the civilians that will benefit," said Jane.

"We all have to pull together at this point. There's no way any of us can let the New Order change how we live. And I for one am not going to stand around and allow them to hunt down good men and woman like it's a day of sport at the range. This will end. One way or another," said Charlie.

~ ~ ~

Jane stripped down to a light T-shirt and bike shorts for bed as Sam lay watching her. He loved to watch her getting ready for bed, even in their current situation. She had rituals he would never really understand, nor would he ever try. He just loved knowing they were together. She turned off the light and nuzzled next to him in the creaky foldout bed.

"I'm not sure this pullout couch is an improvement over the ground," she said.

"Me neither. I think I've been impaled by an errant spring," said Sam.

Jane giggled softly. "I love you, and I know we'll get through this. I'm just worried about Lea."

"Me too. I wish we had some heavier weapons," said Sam. "I get the impression Charlie might have a few loaners, but I hate to ask. He's done enough already."

"When we get home, we have everything we need. We'll grab Lea and some supplies before heading up to the Clark HQ."

"You aren't seriously thinking of joining them right away, are you?"

"Of course I am. Why wouldn't I?" responded Jane.

"We need to find a place where we can hide until this blows over. The last place I want to be is in the middle of a war zone. The HQ might be safe now, but wait until the fighting starts. You saw the New Order guys riding in the back of the truck. Those are people who have no intention of going quietly."

"I'm worried about it too, but I have a duty to my fellow officers."

"And to your family," Sam reminded her.

"And to my family," she said. "But you heard Charlie. This isn't going away on its own. We have to band together and fight back, or we'll never get our lives back. They're hunting cops. It's only a matter of time before they find me."

"I get all of that, but if this whole mess was caused by an EMP—things could be far from normal for a very long time. We might need to consider finding shelter, gathering our resources and looking after ourselves. That includes getting to a place where those thugs can't find us," said Sam.

"Okay, let's not make any decisions right now. We first need to get home and see what we're dealing with."

"I agree."

Sam kissed the top of Jane's head and gently stroked her hair, trying to calm himself enough to fall asleep. They had another long day ahead.

— 14 —

Johnny Evans carried a tray of warm water, tequila and snacks into the Porter police station's conference room. Candles and flashlights illuminated the motley crew of hard-looking ex-prisoners seated around the conference table. Since being "recruited," Johnny had become their slave. Cleaning up their excrement after the toilets failed, serving them food and doing anything else they wanted— including things he would rather not think about.

Johnny couldn't escape because he couldn't leave his grandma behind. She wouldn't survive the hike to the various safe houses, and her supplies were running very low. If things did not change quickly, the meager food he stole from his captors would not be enough to sustain her.

Trying to help the police while keeping his grandma alive gave Johnny a sense of purpose for the first time in his life. His grandma, Ruth, had raised him when his mom died of an overdose. He would keep doing whatever it took to feed her and keep her safe until real help arrived. Relaying information and assisting in the escape of the Porter PD and veterans was the only real way he could fight back against the New Order and keep his grandma safe—as long as he was careful.

On this particular night, it seemed the *jackals*, the name he secretly called his captors, were planning something bigger than usual. Trying to figure out the details of their upcoming plot would require him to linger a little longer than wanted—to listen in to their conversation. He took longer than needed to quietly arrange the refreshments, then checked the garbage, all while trying not to be noticed.

"We need to check it out, man, that's all I'm saying," said a heavily tattooed man named Carl.

"Shit is going down. I know the pigs are planning something," said a man with a deep red scar across his neck.

"I say later tonight we make a little visit to—" started the man who appeared to be in charge. "What the fuck are you looking at, chump?"

Carl pointed at Johnny, freezing him in place.

"Nothing, just bringing food and drinks is all," stammered Johnny.

"Get the fuck out of here before I decide I need more than a drink, bitch," said the leader, to a round of laughter.

Johnny scrambled out of the room. He'd heard enough of their plan to know that he needed to warn Charlie.

— 15 —

Jane stretched out on the lumpy sofa bed. She was convinced the bed had done her back more harm than good. Reaching a hand across the mattress to wake Sam, she realized for the first time that she was alone.

"Sam?" she called out into the predawn darkness.

No answer. The bed creaked as she reluctantly lifted herself off the saggy frame. Muffled talking came from outside the room, reminding her of her current location. Sam and Charlie stood in the candlelit kitchen, talking.

"You go ahead and take this one. We have a second," said Sam, handing Charlie a portable water filtration system.

"Are you sure?" asked Charlie.

"Yeah, we can't leave you here knowing you're drinking water from your tub," said Sam. "We didn't use it on the trip, so it should give you close to a thousand liters of micro-filtered water. You can even hook it right up to your CamelBak and pump water right out of a pond—or your bathtub."

"I wouldn't recommend that," said Jane, turning their heads. "Did I miss anything?"

"No, we were just going over the map again. And I

gave Charlie one of our Katadyn filters. The smaller one," said Sam, kissing her forehead.

"Where did all of this come from?" asked Jane, waving her hand in the direction of the table.

A small assortment of military-grade weapons sat piled on the small table. Three magazine-fed rifles with a hodgepodge of tactical attachments; two identical-looking, standard police-issued M4s with front vertical grips and EOTech sights; and several pistols, mostly Glocks. The array also included two suppressors, which looked like they were sized for rifles.

"It all came from Evansville. The non-police-issue items came from the evidence locker. The chief tried to spread out the weapons to as many of us as possible. I've been issuing them to the individuals I escort to the safe house trail. Jane, you should take one of the department-issued M4s. I know you've trained on them enough to make a difference in a gunfight. Sam should carry this short-barreled rifle," he said, lifting one of the smaller rifles. "The barrel is threaded to take one of the suppressors, just in case."

"Just in case of what?" said Sam.

"I don't know. You might run into someone that needs to be taken down quietly," said Charlie. "I'll also give your traveling companion a rifle. You can swap and switch rifles all you want, based on the situation, but from this point forward, I think you should have these ready at all times. Sam is good to go with an AR-15 platform, right?"

"He can outshoot me with a rifle," said Jane. "Pistols are a different story."

"She's right about that. Does this leave enough for your protection?" asked Sam.

"I'm good. I took one of the better rifles in the evidence locker. One fitted for a suppressor. We grabbed it in a drug bust last month, and I've been eyeballing it ever since. It's better than anything the department will buy us. I'll be just fine." Charlie smiled.

"I was wondering where you got the suppressors," said Jane.

"Chief had us go through the evidence locker and destroy the paperwork with the names of the confiscating officers. He also had us collect some of the more useful pieces of hardware." Charlie winked.

"Finally, we get to play on an even field with the bad guys. I hope none of this is necessary, but super glad to have it all the same. Okay, if you guys are almost finished here, I'll gather up our things and we should be ready to roll," said Jane.

Jane went back to the small room. Packing took only a minute, but she found herself lingering. A strong dose of conflicted feelings arose in her. She desperately wanted to get home to Lea. On the other hand, she knew the situation outside this house was the most dangerous one she had ever experienced. Sam slowed her down considerably. For a split second, she considered asking Sam to stay back with Charlie. He could help ferry people to the trail. She dismissed the idea just as quickly. He'd never leave her side, and like Jane, he'd never accept staying behind when Lea was in danger. Heaving the pack onto her small frame, she walked out of the bedroom, wary of what the day would bring.

— 16 —

Charlie led Sam and Jane north through the crowded woods. The darkness slowed their progress significantly, the uneven terrain causing each of them to frequently stumble for footing over the soft bed of the still forest.

Once they reached the rendezvous location, Charlie sat hunched in the low brush near Jane and Sam, waiting for whomever he was to escort to the horse trail. The waiting bothered him the most. Knowing that the rendezvous location was just outside of town, not far from the gang's center of activity, made Charlie extremely uncomfortable each time he had to do it. After this one, they would have just one more police officer to move out of town. Many of the remaining vets were already in hiding within and around Porter.

A provisional clandestine military force had been quickly assembled by a recently retired Marine master sergeant. The veterans planned to jump into action once the cops started pushing into town. Dividing the New Order with a surprise attack from the inside would hopefully spell the difference between winning and losing the battle. Charlie would be relieved to leave Porter, with the remaining officer, and head for the safety of the provisional HQ. Being the first safe house in the chain as well as the forward communications hub put him in a particularly vulnerable position.

A slight rustling in the brush caused the small group to tense. Both Charlie and Jane held their rifles in the ready position. Sitting back-to-back, they were prepared for any surprise coming their way. Sam served as their over-watch, scanning the shadowy landscape with his binoculars for movement.

Charlie's earpiece crackled, relaying Johnny's voice from the radio handset secured in one of his vest pouches. Johnny had broken protocol, which meant there might be a bigger problem in Porter. They usually communicated late at night, when the gang members were either drunk or passed out—too far gone to notice the radio traffic.

"Charlie…Johnny…get…coming."

"This is Charlie. Repeat. Over," said Charlie in a loud whisper.

"Get…Over," repeated Johnny through the thick static.

The radio went silent moments before a twig snapped nearby, causing the group to shift all of their weapons toward the sound.

"Whoa! It's Mike Sparr," hissed a scared-looking man, with his hands in the air.

A young, exhausted-looking girl stood mostly behind him, tugging on his loose-fitting shirt. Charlie didn't know Mike Sparr by sight, but this had to be him. He'd been told to expect a father and daughter. If this was a trick, it was a desperate one.

"I didn't mean to sneak up on you, but I didn't even know you were here until you started whispering. I didn't even hear you approach. We've been here for about an hour," said the man. "I'm supposed to tell you that your mother sent me and that you like pie, or something like that."

"That's the code," said Charlie. "What's your daughter's name?"

"Jenny," said Mike, nudging her gently forward. "Say hi to our new friends."

"Hi, Jenny," said Sam, kneeling down at her level. "Is this your dad?"

"Honey," snapped Jane.

The little girl hugged the man, nodding her head.

"Good enough for me," said Sam.

"Sorry about that. We can't be too careful," said Charlie, letting his rifle hang on its sling. "This is Sam and Jane Archer. Jane is Evansville PD."

"I completely understand. Mike Sparr, Porter PD," he said, offering his hand.

Jane shook his hand and said, "Sorry about everything that's happening in Porter."

Glancing at Jenny, Mike said, "Yes, but we're going on a hike to a place where we'll be safe."

Picking up Mike's hint, Jane smiled and nodded. "That's right. With hot chocolate and some other treats."

Jenny shifted uncomfortably. Her dirty, matted hair clung to the sides of her pale face. The simple shorts and T-shirt she wore hung on her slight frame and revealed a sustained period of calorie deprivation.

"Daddy, can we eat now? I'm hungry," protested Jenny in a mousy voice.

"In a little while, honey. Right now, we need to start on our adventure through the woods," replied Mike.

"Actually, I brought some food for you, Jenny. Here

are some crackers and nuts mixed with raisins. Eat as much as you want," said Charlie, handing her a plastic bag from one of his cargo pockets.

"Can I, Daddy?" Jenny asked, turning to Mike.

Mike glanced up at Charlie with surprised relief. "Are you sure?"

"Absolutely," stated Charlie.

"Sure, baby. Go ahead," said Mike softly.

"I think we should start on the trail before the sun comes all the way up," said Sam.

"Just keep following the trail, like I said," said Charlie, pointing north into a smallish opening in the trees and thick underbrush. "The horse trail is barely visible from here. If you keep heading due north, moving at a normal walking pace, you should get to Doris's house well before dinner."

A bright orange sunrise poked through the trees to the east. Charlie sensed that none of them actually wanted to move onto the uncertainty of the trail.

"Give me a shout tonight, after midnight, advising me of your location," said Charlie.

"Will do," said Sam.

Jane stepped forward and hugged Charlie.

"Thank you," was all she managed to say. "Watch yourself out here."

"This is my backyard," said Charlie. "I got it covered."

Mike extended a hand to Charlie. "Thanks, man. It is really amazing what you guys in Evansville are doing," said Mike.

"We're in this together," he said before kneeling in front of Jenny. "You take care of your dad out there, and make sure to listen up good. You're safe now."

Jenny nodded solemnly, barely forming a thin smile.

"Catch you all later," he said. "Stay quiet on the trail."

Charlie leaned against a thick tree, watching the small group vanish into the woods, headed toward the horse trail. Although accustomed to living alone, Charlie welcomed the break from his solitude. Having Jane and Sam in the house had allowed him to relax his guard, just slightly. Knowing two extra sets of ears and eyes were in the house went a long way to ease his stress. Charlie turned and walked pensively in the direction of his house. Alone once again with his thoughts.

Johnny's communication had deeply unsettled him. Johnny wouldn't risk communicating during the morning hours unless it was important. Charlie knew he would have to wait until midnight to inquire about the communication. It promised to be a long day.

— 17 —

Johnny sat in the deserted Porter PD communications center, trying to contact Charlie. Either Charlie had his handheld turned off, or it went dead. *Damn.* The *jackals* would be awake soon, shaking off their hangovers. He couldn't count on being alone in the communications room for much longer. If they found him, they would kill him, or worse.

"Charlie, this is Johnny. Do you read? Over."

"Charlie, this is Johnny. Are you there? Over."

He glanced over his shoulder at the door before trying one last time.

"Charlie, you have to get out. They are coming for you. CHARLIE! GET OUT!" Frustrated, he shouted a little too loud.

"What the fuck do you think you're doing?" said a deep male voice from behind him.

Johnny reflexively gripped the handset. He hoped the man who had just entered the room had not overheard his message. As he turned, he moved his hand casually over the power button and secretly pressed down, turning off the main power to the communications panel.

"Nothing. Just messing around. I finished everything I needed to do and was killing time," said Johnny, attempting to look nonchalant.

He desperately sought to keep the guilt off his face. His grandma told him he made a terrible liar. Something about his eyes or voice gave him away. He couldn't recall what she had said, so he generally made it a point to never lie.

"Whatever you're doing, it's over now. Get outta here and go make me something to eat," said the man known as Brown.

"Right away, Brown. I'll find you something good for breakfast," said Johnny.

He moved as quickly as possible without running. Brown had the power to put him behind one of the trucks, like so many that had come before him. He could never allow that to happen—for his grandmother's sake.

Moving out of the communications room, Johnny wondered if Charlie had heard his desperate calls. The New Order men were on their way to Charlie's house, with orders to bring him back for a "visit" with the Boss. No one lived through a "visit" with the Boss.

— 18 —

Charlie hiked back to his house as fast as possible given the low light conditions. Johnny's desperate voice echoed in his head. *What was he saying? Why did he risk a daytime message? What could be so urgent?* When the pieces snapped together, Charlie stopped abruptly. A strong feeling of foreboding overcame him. Years of police work had taught him to trust those feelings. In the field, trusting one's instincts could make the difference between life and death.

Moving slowly from one concealed point to the next, Charlie worked his way in the direction of his home. About fifty yards away, he climbed a sturdy oak and watched his house. Paranoia might be getting the better of him, but he had no intention of being proven correct. Something was off. He could feel it.

Just after he settled into the crook of one of the tree's thick, lower branches, a large dusty pickup truck barreled down his driveway. *Shit.* Charlie watched five heavily armed men offload in his driveway, rushing toward the house. They kicked in the front door and poured inside, shooting immediately. For the next several seconds, they fired bullet after bullet, shattering the first-floor windows and splintering the siding. They moved rapidly through the house, pausing briefly to reload before destroying the next room.

Anger consumed him while he nestled closer to the safety of the oak. He was tempted to open fire on them when they returned to the pickup truck, but his position balanced on a branch was tenuous, especially against multiple shooters—and he didn't dare drop from the tree to look for a better position. If anyone was watching the front of the house, they might see him hit the ground. He'd have to stay put and watch them shoot his house to pieces.

— 19 —

The horse trail consisted of a barely worn path in most spots, indicating that stretches of it hadn't been used in years. At other points along the trail, the path was deeply worn and easily discernable. They exercised caution in these more frequently traveled areas. Mike Sparr was relieved to be walking the path with Jane and Sam Archer. He had dreaded the thought of traveling to the safe house with just Jenny at his side.

Over the past two weeks, Mike and Jenny had moved from one neighbor's home to another. They had hidden in basements, closets, attics and root cellars during the almost daily home searches conducted by the New Order. Their speedy retreat into hiding didn't afford them the luxury of packing more than a school-sized backpack for the ordeal. Showing up empty-handed to the homes of his brave neighbors didn't sit well with Mike. His neighbors were not only sharing precious resources, but also risking their own lives to shelter them. He vowed to return every kindness to the people of Porter, one way or another—and to repay the New Order for the atrocities they'd committed.

Jenny and Mike had moved to Porter just two years earlier, after his wife, Carol, died suddenly of pancreatic cancer. Mike thought Jenny would enjoy their new life away from the memory of hospitals and funeral flowers. Until two weeks prior, the move had done them both good. Mike had excelled in his academy training and enjoyed the sense of purpose gained from being a patrol officer. Jenny, on the other hand, made so many new friends in Porter anyone would have thought they were locals, despite having no family in the area. The community had treated him like one of their own from the start—all the way to this bitter end. He'd never forget that.

Glancing at Jenny's tired face, Mike said, "Can we take a five-minute breather?"

Since starting on the path, Jane had kept the group moving at a tight clip. He appreciated that she had a daughter to return to but knew there was no way either he or Jenny would be able to keep up the pace for the long haul.

"Sure. How about if we grab seats on this fallen tree?" suggested Sam, pointing.

For just a split second, Mike thought he caught an annoyed look from Jane. It was too quick to be sure.

"How much further, Daddy? I'm tired," whined Jenny.

Sam looked at his watch and then the sky. The late morning sun streamed through the dense canopy of the forest. Even though they sat in a shaded spot, the heat and humidity clung to their bodies. The musical chatter of birds continued, undeterred by the heat.

"We probably have another four to five hours of hiking. Give or take," said Sam.

"I appreciate you keeping track of where we are and

how far we have to go. Without the two of you we'd be lost," said Mike.

Glancing at Jane, Sam said, "Well, we've experienced our share of being lost. It's how we stumbled into Charlie. We thought we were headed in the direction of his house but didn't realize how far off we were until he jumped us."

"He was waiting for Officer Seits when we walked into him," said Jane, before she recalled Mike's relationship with Seits. "Sorry."

Mike's head hung low at the memory of Robert Seits. He knew Seits had been taken from the Cooper home and paraded around town before being killed. What he did not know was what had happened to the Coopers. Other families had been killed for assisting runners. The New Order men had no problem executing the entire family, kids included. The message sent to the town was loud and clear. Anyone sheltering cops or veterans would be assassinated. Jenny's friend Melissa was a Cooper. For Jenny's and Melissa's sakes, he hoped the New Order had changed tactics.

Turning to Jenny, Mike said, "You about ready to go, honey?"

"Do we have to? Can't we stay a little longer?" asked Jenny.

"It's fine. A little longer shouldn't hurt our progress," said Sam.

Mike was relieved by Sam's willingness to give Jenny a little longer of a break. However, he could not help but notice that same flash of annoyance cross Jane's face. He stroked Jenny's frail back. Annoyed or not, Mike now didn't care. He would always put his daughter before everyone. Jenny had been through enough between her mom's death, relocation and now all of this? If she needed a ten-minute break, she would get it.

— 20 —

Charlie waited an hour after the New Order truck pulled out of his driveway before climbing down the tree. His body ached from its awkward position on the branch while watching the New Order men destroy his house.

Arriving at the house, Charlie paused at the destruction in front of him. The men had torn through his belongings with a vengeance. Beyond the obvious damage from the excessive gunfire, the sofas were slashed, the televisions thrown to the floor, and dishes shattered and scattered throughout the kitchen. Everything had been turned over, from what he could tell. And that wasn't the worst of it.

A strong scent of ammonia hung heavy in the air from the numerous urine stains on the walls and furniture. One of the men had left a floating brown gift in the last remains of drinking water in his bathtub. *Assholes.* The last couple of cans of food Charlie needed to get him through the next day or two were gone, too.

The steps creaked under Charlie's feet as he descended the basement stairs. When he stepped on the last step, he thought with a mean smile, *Hope one of you assholes tripped.*

The makeshift communications setup he'd used to

75

ferry the brave men and women in blue to safety had been completely smashed. Fortunately, Charlie still had the handheld CB in his backpack. This would allow him to remain in touch with the Porter base. He needed to let Marta know that his time in Porter had come to an end. The men who did this knew where he lived and had likely figured out he was more than just a regular civilian. His safety depended on getting as far from his house as possible. This wouldn't be the last trip they made to Charlie's house. The last police officer hiding in Porter would have to wait until he figured something else out.

Just as he was about to make his way back upstairs, he realized that he'd failed to check the gun lockers. Two massive gun lockers stood in the corner of the room. Over the years Charlie had become a gun enthusiast, or an addict—however you wanted to look at it. He never met a gun he didn't like and rarely let a good deal pass him by. Although he'd showed Jane and Sam the weapons he'd collected from the Evansville PD, he didn't tell them about his personal stash.

Clearly the New Order men knew what was inside the lockers. Even if they couldn't surmise the extent of his personal arsenal, they knew something of value was safely locked away. The exterior finish on the lockers showed the tremendous effort that the men had gone through to get inside. The doors sustained gouges, nicks, dents and deep scratches; however, neither of the industrial-grade safes had given in to their efforts. Both remained firmly bolted to the cement floor and wall.

The heavy-duty locks and steel-reinforced doors were impenetrable through normal means. Only a blowtorch and crowbar could possibly break open the doors. Even with a blowtorch, getting into the lockers was not guaranteed. *Glad I spent the extra change for these babies,* he thought, patting the side of one locker.

Charlie realized with sudden panic that New Order's inability to gain access to the gun lockers made it imperative that he leave the house as quickly as possible. They were likely searching town for the tools needed to open the lockers. Once they acquired the necessary tools, they'd be back. It was only a matter of time. The New Order had access to the entire town. Every repair shop and backyard toolshed lay at their disposal. They could even force the local locksmith to break open the locks. He needed to move, fast.

Charlie pulled a small set of keys from his pants pocket and quickly opened both lockers. His entire arsenal lay in front of him. Several World War II-era rifles and carbines, painstakingly restored to working order, stood in stark contrast to a few modern, AR-style rifles chambered in both 5.56mm and 7.62mm NATO; hunting rifles of different calibers, with their own carefully zeroed scopes; shotguns, both pump action and semiautomatic; break-open barrel shotguns for hunting or skeet shooting; and then the pistols. Charlie had at least a dozen pistols, both revolver and semiautomatic models.

Moving all of the weapons would be a challenge, but leaving the arsenal behind was not an option. Then there was the ammunition to consider. Eventually, the New Order would break in to the lockers, giving them a substantial advantage in the inevitable fight when the police returned. He'd hoped to use these weapons to arm more of the veterans or civilians willing to retake Porter. He had no choice but to hide the entire arsenal.

Charlie moved quickly. He pulled out several black firearm-carrying bags of different sizes and types, which had been tossed on the floor and covered with a toppled shelf. Stuffing the bags to their maximum capacity took Charlie several minutes. Heaving one bag at a time over his shoulder, he lumbered up the basement stairs and out the back door to ferry the items to a safe hiding place.

When Charlie bought the house, he'd walked every square inch of his property, proud of his first home purchase. Toward the back property line, he'd discovered a little rock outcropping that formed a shallow cave on the lower side of the sloped terrain. In the winter he would check the shallow cave for sleeping bears. Now he would stuff it with weapons. He fit the first bag snugly into the back of the cave and then returned for the rest of the bags, knowing his time was quickly running out.

After securely hiding the bags filled with guns and ammunition in the cave, Charlie took one last look around his home for anything useful. The New Order had picked the house clean. Anything that could be used to survive was taken. All the batteries, candles, waterproof clothes and shoes were gone. The rest was destroyed.

Originally reluctant to accept the water filtration unit from Sam, Charlie was now grateful for the help. Having the ability to make fresh water from the creek would be vital to keeping him hydrated and able to move as fast as possible. He needed to catch up with Jane Archer and the others. If the New Order put the pieces together and discovered the trail, they could be actively searching for Jane's group. At the very least, he knew they'd be searching for him. Putting as much distance as possible between himself and the New Order was essential.

— 21 —

Paul Reed hated his current predicament. Stuck in this shitty car with Jack Reilly was not his idea of a career-enhancing situation. The Boss had said he could use a guy like Paul to help patrol the "outer perimeter." The Boss talked like he was some sort of general instead of a punk like the rest of them. Punk or not, Paul wanted to advance in the New Order, and riding with Jack was not going to do it for him. The guy was as dumb as a bag of rocks.

"Pull over, shithead. I need to take a dump," said Paul.

"What? Now? It's almost time for the end of our shift. Can't it wait?" asked Jack.

"No, it can't wait, you dumb fuck. I have to shit."

Jack maneuvered the old Chevy Impala off the road, onto the shoulder.

"Turn off the engine. The Boss said we need to conserve fuel," ordered Paul.

"Really? I'll roast in here without the air on. Hurry it up out there," said Jack, lowering the windows before turning off the engine.

Slamming the car door behind him and walking off the

road into the woods, Paul jabbed his middle finger into the air.

~ ~ ~

Paul needed privacy to do the deed. He wasn't one of those guys who could just drop his trousers and go anywhere—especially for the deuce. Wading into the dense forest through considerable underbrush took more effort than he had expected. *Maybe I should have waited.*

After searching for a few minutes, he found a rock he could use as a makeshift toilet. Sitting quietly in the woods, different layers of the forest's sounds echoed closely. The chatter of birds, the rustle of leaves and the sway of heavy branches filled the spaces around him. Then he thought he heard something out of place. *Was that a child's voice?*

Zipping his pants quickly, Paul silently moved through the forest toward the sound. About a hundred yards away, in the opposite direction of the road, he spotted a small group consisting of two men, a lady and a kid. *Runners.* Better than runners. One of the guys looked like a copper. The hair was growing out, but he could still tell the guy had the *cop top.* Nobody fooled Paul.

He became giddy at the prospect of delivering the four of them to the Boss. He would be promoted instantly, no longer forced to drive around aimlessly with that idiot Jack. For a few moments, he considered fetching Jack to help. He didn't want to mess this up. The more he thought about it, the less he liked the idea. Jack was more likely to screw up the opportunity than not.

Releasing the safety on his pistol, Paul rounded the tree concealing his location and shouted, "Get on the ground, all of you!"

The group was stunned and slow to follow his instruction.

"Now!" he screamed.

"We're just trying to get home, no need for violence," said the older guy.

"Shut the fuck up and get down!"

"You can have anything you want. We have no problem with you and…" said the copper as he quickly clawed at the kid, trying to move her to the ground.

The little girl stood unmoved by the copper's attempts to get her onto the ground under him. Then the kid started screaming. The high-pitched anxious shrill angered Paul. The screaming grated on his nerves and the dude with the cop top was doing next to nothing to shut her up.

The kid would have to go first. No sense in hauling her back with that mouth going nonstop. The Boss hated kids, anyway, and Paul could not stand the noise for another second. He walked closer to the girl, aiming his pistol at her thin chest. *Fucking loudmouthed runt.*

— 22 —

Charlie's feet burned, and his back muscles twitched from the heavy pack and the additional ammunition for his rifle. He'd moved so fast for the past forty-five minutes that he barely had time to register the pain in his body. Unfortunately, stopping wasn't an option. Not if he wanted to catch up with Jane and warn them that the New Order might have additional scouts out looking for runaways.

Looking ahead of him on the trail, Charlie caught a glimpse of Jenny's pink shorts through the dense brush. Just as he was about to call out, Jenny let out the loudest scream he had ever heard. Moving several feet forward on the trail, more of the scene unfolded. Jane and Sam lay facedown on the ground with their hands laced behind their heads; Mike was on his knees, trying to push Jenny to the ground. Something was going down.

Charlie pulled the suppressed rifle across his chest in the ready position as he entered the forest and quickly closed the distance to the group from the concealment of the trees. A short, overweight man with a smooth shaved head materialized beyond the brush, looming over the

82

group and yelling. He pointed a pistol at Jenny, and his screaming intensified. *Where are the others? Are there more New Order men in the vicinity?*

Before he could formulate a plan, the man moved with obvious intention toward Jenny, his pistol hand extending further. It was a pattern Charlie had seen before on the streets. The man was moments from pulling the trigger. Charlie beat him to it, sending three bullets into the man's upper body. The snapping sound of suppressed gunfire faded, replaced by Jenny's frantic screams. Charlie ran to the group as quietly as he could. Mike threw himself over his daughter's body as Jane scrambled to her feet and knocked the stunned man onto his back, disarming him in seconds. The man stared up at Jane and helplessly sputtered blood through his lips, unable to speak. Jane stood a few feet away from the dying man, her rifle pointed at his forehead.

"Are there others?" asked Charlie, arriving next to the group.

"Not sure. He just came out of nowhere," said Jane.

"I'm going to search the area. He can't be alone," said Charlie, moving quickly.

"I'm coming with you," offered Jane.

"I'll watch him. Jenny, stay down," whispered Mike, prying himself from the trembling Jenny.

"Be careful," was all Sam could think to say, glancing at the dying man who had become their prisoner.

Moving carefully through the forest, Jane and Charlie quietly searched for other New Order men. They headed in the direction of the road, correctly assuming the men drove to their location. They both stopped and listened when glimpses of the pavement appeared in the distance. Music softly played. Someone was singing and drumming the music's beat in a low thump. He scanned from left to right, finding the car beyond the heavy forest scrub. Charlie approached the driver's side of the car as Jane moved behind the car and headed to the passenger side in a low crouch. They pounced at once, applying the full force of their training.

"Hands where I can see them!" shouted Charlie.

The surprised man instantly complied, placing his hands on the dash. Jane quickly opened the passenger door, inspecting for weapons.

"Clear!" she shouted.

"Get out of the car and lie flat on the ground," ordered Charlie.

The man started to follow his directions, but before he fully exited the car, Charlie placed the end of the suppressor against the side of the man's head and pulled the trigger. The man dropped to the sun-scorched pavement with a heavy thud. A thick line of blood flowed quickly from his still head. He hadn't intended to execute the guy a moment ago. It had been a last millisecond decision. One he didn't regret.

"Charlie! What the hell?" yelled Jane.

"They found my house, Jane. Came in guns blazing. New Order is onto us, and they won't hesitate to kill us. That guy back there was about to shoot Mike's little girl. The rules have changed. We can't take any chances with people like this. Right now, we need to get this car off the road fast before they see it and send more men to hunt us down," said Charlie. "They'll find the horse trail and send ATVs after us."

"Shit. Alright. We can drive it over in that direction and hide it in the woods. Looks like we can push it far enough off the side to keep casual observers from spotting it. Unless you think we can drive out of here?" asked Jane, hopeful for the ride.

"I thought of that, but we're way safer in the woods. The road leaves us no way to hide, and the only vehicles on the road belong to the New Order. It's only a matter of time before we're spotted in the car. We can keep the keys for later and return for the car when possible. I'll ask Sam to set a waypoint on his handheld GPS so we can find the car later," said Charlie.

"What do you want to do with him?" asked Jane.

"Let's get him into the woods and cover him up. By the time the animals start pulling him apart, we'll be long gone."

"Okay. I'll grab his feet," Jane said urgently.

They carried the man about fifteen yards along the side of the road and hid him deep in the forest, where they heaved him into a tangle of bushes and saplings. When they got back to the car, Charlie pointed at the blood.

"We need to clean that up," said Charlie.

Jane searched the car, producing a dirty pair of jeans. "This'll have to do."

After she wiped up the blood, they dumped a few handfuls of dirt from the shoulder of the road on the stain, spreading it around with their boots to absorb the remaining blood. Charlie examined their handiwork. It would pass muster from a moving car.

"Good enough," he said.

She nodded, throwing the blood-soaked jeans into the thick brush.

"Doesn't look like the past two weeks have caused these guys to lose weight," commented Jane.

"Yeah, well, these guys stole the entire town's food

and basically gorged on it like there was no tomorrow while the rest of us starved."

"Assholes," said Jane as they moved back to the car.

"You put it in neutral and I'll push," said Charlie.

A few minutes later, with the car nestled between two trees and covered with broken branches, they headed back to the group.

"Did you find anything?" asked Mike.

"Yes, but it's no longer a threat. Ever," said Charlie, in a tone that did not invite questions.

— 23 —

The small group regained their momentum on the trail after the near disaster, walking swiftly in the direction of the safe house. Sam and Jane tried to walk hand in hand, but most of the trail was too narrow for two people to pass shoulder to shoulder. Instead, the occasional touch sufficed. Jane needed to recalibrate. She also needed a moment in Sam's arms to forget what she'd just seen and to somehow feel safe again. It frustrated her not to be able to talk freely with Sam. However, she knew that Jenny had been through enough, and talking about what just happened would not do anything to help Jenny's situation. They'd have time to talk as adults when they reached the safe house.

"How are you holding up?" she asked Sam.

"Shaken—not stirred," said Sam, eliciting a quick chuckle.

"He just came out of nowhere. We were totally unprepared. Just sitting there drinking water like a bunch of day hikers," she said.

"We got lucky again, thanks to Charlie," said Sam.

"I know. Next time, it might not work out in our favor."

"There won't be a next time. We get Lea and get out. Simple enough," said Sam, always the optimist.

"Yeah, simple enough."

"I'm going to check on Charlie," said Sam.

Leading the group, Jane tried her best to keep them moving while being mindful of Jenny's size and ability to travel.

~ ~ ~

Sam walked near the end of the line just in front of Charlie, who brought up the rear. While working as an emergency medical responder, Sam had seen his share of men die as a result of violence. Fortunately, he never actually saw the violence that caused the dying. Thoughts of Lea raced through his mind, intermixed with the memory of the man's death song. The thud as the man hit the ground and the deep gurgling and whistling sounds that escaped the man's lungs as he struggled for his last breaths. He'd unceremoniously died moments after Jane and Charlie left to search for the rest of the New Order crew. The sight of it haunted him.

Charlie looked just as shaken. Sam read Charlie as the kind of guy who was everyone's friend, a serious but kind man. Although Sam didn't see what had happened when Charlie and Jane found the other New Order man, he did see the blood splatter on Charlie's shoes. Sam was relieved to have Charlie traveling with the group, even if it meant the New Order might be trailing them. The police officer understood what needed to be done and appeared to have what it took to do it without hesitation.

"You doing okay?" Sam asked over his shoulder to Charlie.

"I've been better. You?" responded Charlie.

"About the same. Do you think that was the last of them?"

"It's hard to know. Either those two were a search party looking for us, or they just stumbled on us," said Charlie.

"I guess we'll never know. Too bad we couldn't have taken their car. A ride would have been great right about now. Air-conditioning wouldn't hurt either," said Sam, wiping the sweat off his brow.

"No kidding. My sweat is sweating. I'm concerned about those two," Charlie said in a low whisper.

Sam glanced down the trail toward Mike and Jenny. Jenny looked like she was in shock. Her face was a clammy white mask of fear, and her eyes were wide open, staring blankly ahead as her little feet plodded along. She hadn't spoken since she'd stopped screaming. Mike half dragged, half carried her. Both looked exhausted and dehydrated.

"Me too. Not much we can do for them. At this point, giving them an easier pace isn't even an option. What happened back there? At your house?" asked Sam.

"New Order basically trashed the place. There was nothing left except the guns in my gun safes. They couldn't get into those. I figured it was just a matter of time before they came back with tools for the job. So I bolted as quickly as possible and basically sprinted to your location."

"Sorry about your house. That was probably tough to see. Who knows what we're walking into when we get back to Evansville. Do you think they were looking for you specifically or just going through houses?"

"I've been wondering that myself. I'm guessing they

were looking for me. Otherwise, Johnny wouldn't have tried to send me a message. I think he tried to warn me that they were coming. It would have been extremely dangerous for him to send that message during the morning hours. He risked everything for me, for us. I hope he didn't get..." Charlie trailed off midsentence.

"Yeah. Me too."

Sam and Charlie continued walking in silence. The sound of their footfalls rang in Sam's ears as a heavy mood blanketed him.

— 24 —

Doris Venture sat contently in her oversized white wicker chair, looking out over her land. Not much had changed since the lights went out for her, except helping the runners. One day, shortly after everything stopped working, a man named Charlie Stout came to her house and told her about the events in Porter. Before Charlie came, Doris thought only her power was out, until she realized her truck also failed to operate. Doris was glad she never made that trip into town. According to Charlie, the New Order men were a nasty bunch. If her car had been working, she would have driven right into the thick of things without even knowing it.

Sitting alone and waiting for more runners every afternoon and evening became her ritual. She was never certain when or if they would come, only that they would be coming. Charlie told her to place a plant on the deck rail if everything was as it should be. Otherwise, the runners would just keep running. Today, the geranium pot sat on the rail of her large Southern-style verandah— a beacon of hope for anyone on the run.

Despite the fact that she'd gotten along by herself for close to a decade, the visitors comforted Doris. She'd forgotten what it was like to have company. Loneliness had become her only companion after Travis, her only child, left for the Marine Corps. She'd sent him to fight for freedom in Iraq ten years ago, and he came home from Iraq a hero—in a closed casket.

His staff sergeant said he died fighting to save his squad during a vicious ambush. He'd rushed off to cover one of their exposed flanks, whatever that meant, and disappeared in a massive explosion. She didn't doubt the story. Her son was always a brave and principled boy, even as a child. He was everything her ex-husband was not. The Marine Corps had been perfect for him, even if it ended the way it did. She was very proud of him.

Charlie told her to hide Travis's picture—something about being safe and the New Order. Doris could not bring herself to remove Travis's picture from the mantel, right next to his framed Bronze Star medal and service ribbons. It was all she had left of her boy.

Doris figured there would be a runner or two anytime now. She was ready with food, fresh water and a comfortable place to sleep for each person that came through. Her extensive garden served her well during this crisis. She had all she needed. The garden produced far more than she could ever eat. Normally she would preserve the remaining harvest, but using her limited fuel to run the generator for canning just didn't seem right. Instead, she dried or pickled much of the produce or gave it to the runners. She had so much food she even gave away the peaches right off the trees from her vast orchard. For the winter, she would eat from her extensive stores of canned food. She often chuckled when people talked about "prepping for survival." *Prepping? Try living on a self-sustaining farm.* She even had a hand pump water well.

It provided all the fresh water she could ever need.

Doris would be just fine as far as food and water were concerned, but providing assistance to the men and women of the Porter Police Department was extremely risky. Charlie had warned her that the New Order men were all convicted felons, who would think nothing of killing her if they found out what she was doing. She didn't care. Travis wouldn't have hesitated to help the men and women in blue. He'd always talked about applying for a job with one of the local police departments if he didn't make the Marine Corps a career. She'd honor his legacy by helping the runners, no matter what the outcome.

— 25 —

Brown sat in the communications room of the former Porter Police Department, scanning the airwaves. As a former Navy radioman, Brown knew how to make the lifeless machine sing for him. He knew that by channel skipping, he would eventually pick up a transmission that would tell him what the cops were doing. The Boss was right, they were up to something, and Brown intended to figure out what they were planning before anyone else did. He'd learned the hard way that information is power, and being the first to know something provided the most power.

That skinny sneak Johnny was also up to something. Brown had caught him communicating with someone— he just could not figure out what Johnny was saying or whom he talked with, if he even made contact. Eventually, everything would come to light. Mistakes would be made, and when they were, Brown would be ready.

After a while, Brown's hands became weary and his eyes tired from sitting at the communications desk. Turning the frequencies and hearing nothing but static began to wear on him. Channel fifty-two, static.

Frequency level C, channel forty-one, had nothing but static. Every channel and frequency he tried, he found static. Then a voice rang out:

"...Marta...come in..."

Mary? Marty? What is she saying? Every time the person repeated the name through the emptiness of static and space, Brown became more furious at his inability to get a clear signal.

"Charlie, this is Marta. Copy?"

Finally, loud and clear.

Marta! Brown froze. He knew that name. *Where did he see that name? Was it here or on the inside? It was definitely here, at the Porter PD headquarters.* Brown recalled seeing a mug with the name Marta written on it in the break room. She'd probably used a Sharpie black marker in an attempt to ward off her coworkers from using her favorite "Shut Up and Stand in Line" mug. This was the break he needed! She must be part of the PD.

"Charlie, you copy? This is Marta. We have one more delivery. Are you ready?" Marta said daringly.

"Charlie? Are you there?" the voice repeated.

Charlie did not reply to Marta's calls.

Brown quickly pieced the puzzle together. The Boss had ordered a raid on the home of a man named Charlie Stout. Turned out he was likely a copper. Although there were no uniforms or other cop paraphernalia, there was a large communications setup in the basement and two large gun lockers. The guys were still trying to get into the lockers.

Those sneaky bastards! thought Brown. They were moving their people out, one at a time, right under our noses. Smiling, Brown realized he had discovered very valuable information. Only one question remained. Who would be the best customer for his information?

~ ~ ~

Marta Rhodes sat in her sweltering attic, trying desperately to contact Charlie. He always gave her several "squawkers" right after successfully launching runners on the trail to the first safe house. A "squawker" consisted of three fast on and off babbles, which sounded like someone trying to talk over static. Charlie had failed to do this after taking delivery of Mike Sparr and his daughter this morning. Then she'd seen the New Order truck headed in the direction of Charlie's house. The truck moved fast, like they had a purpose—which was not a common occurrence for these parasitic thugs.

The sight of them speeding away worried her. They were so close to getting all of the remaining police officers out of Porter. They just needed to get Gayle Jones out. Then Charlie would leave too. She did not look forward to being the only remaining set of eyes in Porter, but someone had to do it. Besides, no one would suspect that "little old Marta" was up to anything. She didn't look like a cop, and as part of the administrative department, she was not listed on the duty roster in the same way. They might find her name somewhere, but so far, she hadn't heard of any serious incidents involving the administrative staff. A few houses had been searched, but that was it. She felt safe, sort of.

She would make one more desperate attempt to contact Charlie, then wait until tomorrow to try again. If she didn't hear from him tomorrow night, she had to assume he was dead, and they'd have to come up with a different plan to smuggle Gayle Jones out of Porter.

"Charlie, you copy? This is Marta. We have one more delivery. Are you ready?" she said into the air.

She knew saying both of their names was prohibited under their rules of communication. However, on occasion she had inadvertently slipped a name or two in without consequence. Those times emboldened her now in her desperation.

Her frantic calls were returned by cold, bare static. Looking out her attic window, Marta suddenly felt very alone.

— 26 —

"Damn it!" muttered Jane as she swatted another feasting mosquito. "At this point, I think more surface area of my skin is covered with bug bites than not."

"Me too," said Sam, scratching his neck. "Next time we go on a backcountry hike, we bring triple the amount of bug spray."

"If there is a next time. I get the feeling we're on a permanent camping trip from this point forward," said Jane.

"How much further, Daddy?" whined Jenny.

Looking at his watch, Mike said, "Not too much longer, honey."

"We're almost there. In fact, I think it would be best if the four of you settle here. Take a break while I run ahead. Doris and I worked out a signaling system to alert runners if it was safe to approach her house. I don't want to walk into a trap," said Charlie.

"You mentioned that we need to look for the flowerpot before coming out of the forest. I'll go with you," offered Jane.

"Okay, let's leave the heavy gear behind so we can travel light and fast," said Charlie.

"We got this covered," said Sam, patting Mike on the shoulder.

"Be back in a few," said Jane. "Stay off the trail while we're gone."

They dropped their packs and jogged down the horse trail due north. When Jane looked back, her husband melted into the forest, dragging the two packs with him.

"Doris's house is just beyond that rise," said Charlie, pointing down the trail. "Let's make our way around those rocks and have a look."

The house sat still in the middle of a vast clearing. A luscious vegetable garden and a barn flanked the serene white farmhouse. Green grass and a peach orchard covered the expanse of the space behind the house. A flowering pink geranium in a cobalt blue pot sat on the porch rail.

"Wow. Nice place. How did you find it?" asked Jane.

"I met Doris at a Porter fire department BBQ last summer. She mentioned she lived on the horse trail. I knew about the horse trail and had gone for long runs on it, but never this far. When the shit hit the fan, I ran until I got here, hoping to find Doris," said Charlie.

"Looks like she's far enough from both towns to keep her out of harm's way."

"That's my hope. Looks like things are fine. That pink geranium is our signal. Let's get the others," said Charlie, motioning to Jane.

She glanced at the porch again, chuckling at the simple signal that could mean the difference between life and death. When they returned, a robust-looking woman with gray hair stood on the covered porch. She walked down the stairs to meet them, obviously alerted to their presence.

"Charlie! Gosh, am I glad to see you," said Doris, in a thickly sweet Southern accent. "I thought I saw something moving on the trail."

"Were we that obvious?"

"No. I've been waiting. Figured it was about time for another group."

Charlie stepped forward and hugged Doris.

"Glad to see you're doing well, Doris. Let me introduce you to Mike and Jenny Sparr. Mike is Porter PD. We also have Jane and Sam Archer. Jane is Evansville PD."

"Evansville PD? Are we moving the Evansville PD out now too?" asked Doris.

"No. They wandered into this mess from a camping trip," said Charlie.

"Where are my manners, please do come in. Make yourselves at home. The more the merrier," said Doris, opening the front door for them.

The group moved into the coolness of the neatly appointed farmhouse. Gleaming pine floors and antique furniture greeted the weary travelers.

"Your house is beautiful!" exclaimed Jane.

"Thank you, dear. I'm kind of partial to it, as you can imagine. I can prepare a nice snack while you all rest. Charlie, you can stay in Travis's room. Mike and Jenny, why don't you take the front room. Jane and Sam can take the blue room in the back. You can get your things settled and wash up. There are fresh water basins in all the rooms," said Doris.

"We're fine. We don't want to use your water for bathing," said Sam, shocked that Doris would offer such a precious commodity.

"Don't worry about that, honey. I have a well with

plenty of water," Doris said proudly. "Take your time and wash as much as you need."

The prospect of washing and eating seemed to revive the exhausted group.

"Doris, I'll wash up and then help you in the kitchen. We have some dried grains we can offer to the group for food," said Jane.

"No need. My garden has done so well this year that I can hardly eat it all fast enough. You all will be doing me a great service by eating your share of the harvest," said Doris.

"Real food! Can we eat, Daddy?" begged Jenny.

"Yes, after we clean up," said Mike.

"Aw…" was the only protest the tired Jenny could muster.

— 27 —

Jane dropped her heavy, dirty backpack onto the pristine wide plank pine floor. The bedroom had an antique cherry wood four-poster bed and a matching bureau. A jug of water sat on the bureau, next to an old-fashioned porcelain washbasin. The lace curtains fluttered silently on a slight breeze, filling the serene blue room with earthy scents.

Stretching out on the bed, Sam sighed. "Wow, does this bed feel nice. I think I'll sleep like the dead tonight."

"Bad analogy, given what we went through today," said Jane.

Jane yanked her sweat-stained T-shirt off and stood at the basin, washing herself with the precious well water. A cake of homemade soap sat beside the washbasin. Jane lathered the bar into a sudsy froth, filling the room with a homey lavender scent. The clean feeling was a welcome change from her usual dirty state.

"Now that we can talk freely, what really happened when you and Charlie found the other New Order guy?" said Sam, moving from the bed to stand behind her.

Jane stopped splashing her face and grabbed a thick white towel to dry herself. She leaned back into Sam's strong arms, allowing herself to close her eyes and forget the day for just a second. After breathing deeply for a moment, she responded, "I'm not even sure where to begin. I'm still trying to process everything."

"That bad?" said Sam. "I figured as much given how the two of you looked when you came back."

"It started off fine. We found the dead guy's partner in a car on the side of the road. Charlie took the driver's side and I approached from the passenger side. We ordered the guy out of the car and onto the pavement, but before he got all the way out of the car, Charlie shot him at point-blank range. He just dropped the guy right there. No warning or provocation. I've never seen anything like it. He put the end of the suppressor against his head and that was it," said Jane.

"Shit. That is bad. But then again, Charlie saved Jenny and the rest of us from the first guy. Who knows what would have happened if he didn't come along. From my vantage point, I think Jenny was just the first to be killed. Who knows what else he would have done to us. I think Charlie's actions are extreme, but also spot on," said Sam. "The rules have changed."

"That's what Charlie said," added Jane. "What really bothers me is that I think he's right, and I'm not sure I could have done the same thing myself. Who knows, I might have tried to drag the guy along with us. I could have endangered all of us," said Jane, rubbing her forehead with her free hand.

Sam led her to the bed, where they took a seat.

"You're a good person and this is an unusually dangerous situation. Charlie has been dealing with this since it started, and he's seen things we can't even begin to imagine. For Christ's sake, just a couple of days ago we were still on a pleasant backpacking trip, oblivious to all of this," Sam reminded her.

"It was just a shock to see everything I thought I stood for evaporate in a second," said Jane.

"Charlie wouldn't have done that unless it was absolutely necessary to keep us safe," said Sam. "We have to trust his judgment."

Jane nodded. "I hope I never reach the point where I could put a gun up to someone's head and pull the trigger."

"It won't come to that as long as we play it safe," said Sam.

"If it does come down to that, I have to be ready to pull the trigger—for you and Lea."

"You are not alone in this. I need to be ready, too," said Sam as he pulled her into him, cradling her in his arms.

Jane closed her eyes and allowed him to hold her a little longer. After a quiet minute, she reluctantly disentangled from Sam's embrace.

"I'm going to help our hostess while you get washed up."

"With your dirty bathwater?" said Sam, followed by a wink and quick kiss on her cheek.

"Slightly used water," she said.

"I stand corrected."

— 28 —

Mike and Jenny sat at the large farmer's table in the kitchen. Looking around the kitchen, Mike guessed that Doris spent most of her time here. The clean white Formica countertops and large white farmer's sink dominated the functional kitchen. Doris appeared to be in her glory, preparing refreshments for them. Her ease and welcoming nature finally persuaded him to relax and enjoy the hospitality. He finally felt like a welcome guest instead of a fugitive relying on handouts.

"Can I have more of this?" asked Jenny, holding up an empty bowl.

"Slow down, princess. At this rate you'll eat Ms. Doris out of house and home," joked Mike.

"Not a chance. You eat as much as you would like, sweetie," said Doris.

"Food has been a bit of an issue for us. We've been living off the generosity of people like you for the past couple of weeks. Generosity most could barely afford. Jenny and I tried to eat as little as possible, so as not to overstay our welcome—if you know what I mean."

"I won't have any of that kind of thinking around

here. My house is your house, and I need hungry mouths to keep it running," she said, taking a seat next to Jenny. "It's hard for me to believe what's happening. I'm so far removed from anything like that here. Nothing has changed for me except I can't watch my shows in the evening. But that's probably for the best. TV rots your brain, right, Jenny?"

"You have a TV? Can I watch it?" Jenny asked excitedly.

"Did I hear someone mention watching TV?" asked Jane while walking into the kitchen.

"Don't we all wish. Can I get you some peach salad, honey?" asked Doris.

"Sure, I would love some, but please let me help," replied Jane.

"No need. I have it all right here," said Doris, scooping a large portion of sweetened peaches from a handmade ceramic bowl.

"Your home is just lovely. How long have you lived here?" asked Jane.

"Almost thirty years. The place is such a part of me, I just can't imagine moving anywhere else. I know in the long run I'll have to move closer to town or maybe hire help for the farm, but right now I'm happy to stay put. Do you live in Evansville?"

"I do. Sam and I live with our daughter, Lea, on the eastern side of town," said Jane.

Mike saw Jane's expression change after she mentioned Lea. Now he understood why she'd pushed them so hard on the trail. It must be killing her inside to be out of contact with her daughter.

"Things are different in Evansville, judging by what we heard. I'm sure she's fine," said Mike.

Jane nodded silently, clearly not wanting to explore the topic any further. An awkward moment passed before Doris broke the silence.

"Jenny, you look like your peach-stuffed face is about to fall sound asleep. Go ahead and take a nice long nap. We won't be having dinner for a couple of hours."

"Sounds like a plan to me. Come on, sweetie. I'll get you settled," said Mike, turning to Doris before getting up from the table. "I really can't thank you enough."

"Seeing her stuffed to the gills with peaches is thanks enough."

~ ~ ~

Charlie waited at the top of the stairs until Doris excused herself to pick some vegetables for dinner. He hoped Jane wouldn't join her. They needed to have a frank discussion, without Doris. When he heard the back screen door slam shut, he descended the stairs and took a seat at the table. He was glad to see Mike and Jenny were gone, too.

"We need to talk about something before Doris returns."

"What's up?" said Jane, pushing the bowl of peaches in his direction.

"Thank you. I'll have some in a minute," he said. "I was just thinking that Doris might not be safe out here anymore."

"What do you mean?" asked Sam.

"Well, my friend Johnny tried to communicate with me right before my house was raided. He must have heard that the New Order was going to hit my home, or he wouldn't have risked a daytime communication. Then we run into those guys on the road, or they run into us, however you want to look at it. It's only a matter of time before they find the car and the bodies."

"And the horse trail," added Jane.

"Exactly."

"Shit. We can't just leave Doris out here alone," said Sam.

"I know. But she won't want to leave. I'm sure of it. And if the New Order is not looking for us on the horse trail, I need to keep Doris in place until the last person is out of Porter," said Charlie.

"Maybe Marta will know more. Can you contact her tonight?" asked Jane.

"I can try, but all I have is the small handheld CB. The range isn't great. The unit is more for close-range communications," said Charlie.

"Maybe Doris has a radio?" asked Sam.

"She might. I never really asked. We never coordinated her accepting runners. They were just instructed that if the plant was not visible on the porch rail, they needed to keep moving. I guess we can ask her. What do you two plan to do from here? This is probably the closest the trail gets to your house."

Looking at Sam, Jane said, "We plan to leave before dawn. Hopefully, we can make it back to Evansville before dinnertime."

"You should plan to take it slow and very careful-like. You might end up going through some populated areas before reaching home," said Charlie.

"Yeah, we're worried about that. Do you have any updates on the current situation in Evansville?" asked Jane.

"All I know is that the cops are gone. We managed to

move everyone out. You will have absolutely no backup out there," said Charlie.

"We'll have to be extremely cautious," said Sam.

"I'm not so sure it's a good idea for you to go back, Jane. The New Order might have figured out you're blue. If they did, they'll be looking for you," warned Charlie.

"We have no choice, Charlie. We have to get Lea out of there," said Jane.

"I know. I'll do everything I can to help you with any supplies or routing information I can provide," said Charlie.

"Thanks, we can use all the help we can get," said Sam.

The trio sat silently in the kitchen. The warm evening sky slowly turned a brilliant orange as the shrill of cicadas filled the space between them.

— 29 —

Sam stirred to the sounds of voices just outside his bedroom window. He had intended to lie down for just a few minutes, but the comfortable bed, cool breeze and sheer exhaustion knocked him into a deep sleep. Upon awakening, he was not exactly sure of his location. *Am I in a hotel? A friend's house?*

"Can we roast marshmallows too!" shouted an excited child.

He recognized the voice, which jumpstarted his brain. They were at a house in the middle of nowhere, waiting for tomorrow. Waiting to get back to their daughter. He opened his eyes to the reality he had briefly forgotten. The light of a roaring campfire shone into the dark bedroom, reminding him of his more immediate need. Dinner. He hurried down to join the others outside.

"Wow, this looks amazing," said Sam.

Kissing Jane on the head, Sam took a seat next to her on a log bench. Everyone lounged around the campfire, anticipating dinner.

"Honey, I could make good food anywhere so long as I have my secret ingredients," said Doris proudly.

"What are those?" asked Mike.

"Well, if I told you, then they wouldn't be a secret, now would they. Jenny, be a dear and pass me those bowls—the campfire stew is ready," said Doris.

Doris passed each person an oversized bowl with roasted potatoes and a hearty stew made in a cast-iron pot suspended over the fire by a tripod. She'd also made some sort of cornbread, although Sam was not too sure how she managed to pull that one off on an open fire. He could not remember being so excited about a meal since he was a child and his mom made the Thanksgiving feast for the entire family.

"Do you think it's okay to have a fire going? Maybe someone will see the smoke and come looking," said Mike.

"It should be fine. Plus, we're so far out of both towns that the likelihood of anyone seeing or smelling the fire is pretty slim," said Charlie.

"I've been lighting fires since the whole thing started, with no problem. In the beginning I had no idea what was happening. I went about business as usual, which included burning all of the scrub I cut from the clearing. Believe me, with the amount of smoke I've been putting out, if they were going to find me, they would've," said Doris.

"This is amazing, Doris. Thanks so much," said Jane, eating a hearty spoonful.

"My pleasure."

"Doris, you don't happen to have any sort of communications devices, like a CB radio or a shortwave radio, do you?" asked Charlie.

"I don't, but Travis did. I haven't really cleaned out all of his things from the shed. He used a section of it for his hobbies. Said he liked some privacy. You know how kids are. I'm pretty sure he had a radio, although I'm not sure it still works."

"You mind if we have a look at it? I need to touch base with Marta in Porter," said Charlie.

"Sure, you go right ahead. There's a separate generator out there too. Again, I haven't needed to use it, so I'm not sure the generator works. But it should. I have a helper come by to cut and chop firewood," said Doris, with a nod toward the extensive row of cut and stacked firewood. "If I recall correctly, he ran the generator to power his chipper, so I think it's probably still fine. Just pull the generator outside and run a line inside. I don't want anyone getting hurt from the fumes."

"Will do, thanks. Is there anything you need us to help you with while we're here? I'm sure you could always use an extra set of hands around the farm," asked Charlie.

"If you don't mind hauling some water from the well into the house, that would be a tremendous help. I have large containers inside. So far I've gotten into the habit of bringing one jug in per day. It would be great to have a little stockpile to give my old bones a break."

"We can do that, no problem," said Mike.

Turning to Charlie, Sam said, "What's your plan for tomorrow? Jane and I will be leaving around the same time we left your house. We would like to get home before dinnertime. Like you said, we have no idea what we're walking into and need to leave extra time in case we need to slow our pace considerably."

"I think we need to leave around the same time, maybe 4:45 a.m. Does that work for you and Jenny?" Charlie said, looking at Mike.

"It sure does. We can be ready when you're ready to leave. I can't tell you how much I appreciate the escort to the next safe house. How far away is it?" asked Mike.

"It's about the same distance as we walked from my house to here. So if all goes well, we should be at the next house before dinner. Then, the following day, we can reach the new HQ," said Charlie.

"That'll work. What does the headquarters consist of?" asked Mike.

"Our chief took over a kids camp on the border between Clark and Grant," said Charlie.

"Sounds decent enough," said Mike.

"It's the safest place around right now. All of the Evansville police and their families are there, along with the officers we got out of Porter. It won't be long until more police departments join the fun. Things are really shaping up to be as comfortable as possible up there until this all blows over," said Charlie.

Finishing his dinner, Sam turned to Mike and said, "How about if you and Jane haul water and clean up while Charlie and I check on the radio?"

"That'll work. Jenny can help with the dishes," said Mike.

"Okay," said a tired Jenny, with a slight yawn.

Leaning toward Mike, Jane said, "I'll be surprised if she makes it up the stairs before falling asleep."

"I won't be far behind her." Mike winked.

~ ~ ~

An old wooden shed sat a few hundred yards from the main house. Sam hadn't noticed it when they'd first walked up to Doris's home or while sitting around the campfire. He stepped inside and turned on the flashlight he'd carried with him for the past two weeks while out camping. The bright LED light illuminated the entire room, exposing its contents.

Doris stored a few riding-type mowers and a surprising number of tools, old and new, in the shed. The tools were neatly arranged on wooden, handmade pegs attached to the inside walls of the building. A heavy wooden potter's table sat against the wall under a row of windows, providing the perfect location for sprouting seeds in the spring to get a jump on the growing season. Doris really did have everything she needed here. Sam admired her preparedness, even if it was accomplished through casual lifestyle choices and not by design.

He found a door leading to another room in the shed. The name "Travis" had been whittled at chest level, indicating that Doris's son had probably carved it as a child. Examining the letters, Sam was sad for Doris. She probably felt the same way every time she saw it, remembering her son as a spirited young child. He pushed open the unlocked door, taking a step inside. Charlie followed closely behind.

"Wow, look at all this stuff." Charlie whistled.

"Yeah, I guess Travis liked his radio," said Sam, taking in the set.

An assortment of electronic parts were strewn across a roughhewn table in front of a CB radio set. At least it looked like it was a CB radio. No telling, since it appeared to be built from scratch. Sam was impressed.

"Looks like the kid built this one, nice job too from the looks of it. No telling if it will work until we get some juice going to it," said Sam. "Looks like he was searching for a part, so I'm guessing I have some work ahead of me."

Sam picked up one of the electronics pieces, blowing a

thick layer of dust into the light.

"Looks like it's been a while since anyone has been in here," said Charlie.

"Yeah. Did you see the generator anywhere?" asked Sam.

"No, I'll check the other side of the shed," said Charlie, moving out of the room.

Charlie stepped into the doorway and scanned his flashlight into the main area of the shed. "I've got it. It's under a tarp. Give me a hand. We need to move it outside."

"Okay, I'll grab a cord and be right with you."

Mercifully, the generator was one of those portable types built into a frame with two wheels on one side. They muscled the heavy generator over uneven terrain to the outside corner of the building near Travis's section of the shed and snaked the cord into the shed through a small window.

"Okay, let's see if this baby works," said Charlie, checking the gas and oil levels.

"I'll go back and see if I can hook up the CB to the generator outlet," said Sam, walking back toward the shed.

Sam moved quickly back into the shed, the light of his flashlight illuminating his path. The fine layer of dust on everything in the small room didn't give him a lot of hope. The radio hadn't been used since Travis was still alive, and based on the Bronze Star citation sitting on Doris's mantel, that meant it hadn't been powered for close to ten years. He had his doubts whether the parts would still function. The weather hadn't invaded the room, but electronics were not meant to sit unused for extended periods of time. However, looking around the shed's ample supply of electronics parts and specialized tools, Sam felt confident that he could fix any problems caused by time. If Travis was able to build the radio from the supplies in this shed, Sam could fix it.

The loud rumble of the generator broke the quiet, drowning out nature's forest symphony with a harsh reminder of the world they once lived in. Although Sam would have preferred that none of this had happened, he had to admit that living without the noise and distractions of the modern world felt kind of nice. Nice in a way that made him imagine living a self-reliant life with Jane and Lea on a rustic farm like this one. Doris didn't seem bothered at all by the current circumstances. There was something to be said about that.

"How is it looking in there?" said Charlie through the window.

"Hold on," said Sam, plugging the power cord directly into an inverter hardwired to the radio.

Sam imagined that Travis had done this before. Probably during a power outage caused by a storm. Sam flipped a switch, powering the radio set. He depressed the transmission button on the handset, but couldn't hear much over the generator. Turning the volume higher didn't seem to help the situation.

"Charlie! Move it back!" shouted Sam.

"Move what back?"

"The generator. Take it around the corner, as far from the window as possible."

Charlie ran from the window and slowly pulled the generator around the side of the shed until the cord pulled taut. The extra distance and redirection of sound away from the window decreased the noise level enough for Sam to hear himself think again.

"How's that?" asked Charlie, walking into the small room.

"Better. The set seems fine, but without anyone signaling, it's hard to know if the unit can send and receive. All I hear right now is static," said Sam.

"Alright. Let's turn everything off and wait another couple of hours until after midnight. Then I can signal Marta. We should be able to figure out if it's working pretty fast," said Charlie.

"I would think so. Given the size of the antenna Travis installed onto the side of the shed, if this thing is working, we should be able to contact Mars."

~ ~ ~

Doris and Jenny stood side by side in front of the large farmhouse kitchen sink. Even though Doris didn't need the help, she loved being in the kitchen with another person by her side. The rhythm of household chores served as a medium for unspoken communication between the two of them.

"If you yawn again, I think you might fall asleep while you're washing," said Doris.

"I'm tired and Daddy said that tomorrow we have to walk out of here to another house. Can't I just stay here?" asked Jenny, sponging off a glass.

Glancing at Mike, Doris said, "I would love it if you could, but this time, you need to keep walking to the next house. It will be fine. Besides, you can always come back to see me. You're welcome anytime, my dear."

"Okay, Daddy, can we come back? I really like it here," said Jenny.

"Sure, honey. After we get settled, we'll come back to

visit Ms. Doris. But for now, I think I need to get you to bed. We have an early start tomorrow. Doris, I'm going to get this zombie child to bed and then I can help you finish."

"No need at all. Jenny and I were able to wash everything. I'm just putting a few things away. You get yourself some rest too. You'll need it for tomorrow. Here, take this flashlight so you can find your way around," said Doris.

"You don't have to ask twice. I could use some shut-eye. Come on, chicken," said Mike, grabbing Jenny's still-damp hand.

The floor creaked in the still farmhouse as Mike and Jenny made their way to their cozy room for the night.

— 30 —

Freddie Jackson, now known respectfully as the "Boss," sat on the front porch of his new house, pumping weights. The house was a "gift" from a Porter family to honor his reign. Not that they had a choice. The Boss and his guys walked into any house they wanted and ordered the people out, and out they went. Those who didn't immediately comply were dealt with harshly, setting an example for the community. It didn't take more than a few examples for people to get the message. He was surprised by just how easy it was to take over the town. The people in Porter never knew what hit them.

The way he saw it, Porter was his reward for the years spent cooped up in that PrisCorp shithole. Not that life had been too bad in prison. Serving a life sentence without the possibility of parole gave a man perspective. The key to serving a life sentence was making a new life on the inside. The Boss managed to reconstruct his "business network" in PrisCorp. Underpaid guards and fellow inmates were more than willing to fill the ranks of his new army. Before he knew it, Freddie Jackson was on top again. The cash and drugs surged through the facility, followed by the perks. The Boss had his own room, willing ladies brought in for visits as much as he requested, and plenty of take-out food. The only thing he lacked was his freedom, which was a big fucking thing.

When the power failed and his door unlocked, he'd sprinted like a fool with the rest of them until he was well clear of the prison. When he realized the lights were out for good, the Boss knew an opportunity had fallen right into his lap. A once-in-a-lifetime opportunity to emerge as a legitimate power, out of the shadows. The days of running a covert network of drug dealers and petty thieves—always looking over his shoulder—was finished. With the army he'd built in the prison, he'd do what all of the great leaders in the past had done. Invade and occupy.

Porter, the closest town, had proven too easy. The cops and locals were too busy trying to figure out what had happened to the lights to fight back. Once they'd captured the police station, the town basically gave up. Still, he didn't need any resistance fighters giving him trouble. He'd read about the resistance groups in World War II, always fucking with the Germans wherever they went. Hunting down all the cops and veterans was the only way to fully establish his new turf. So far, no hero cops had come out of the woodwork to give him trouble. They got the message, along with everyone else.

The rumble of a lone vehicle interrupted his thoughts. A pickup truck pulled into the driveway and four of his "officers" climbed out of the truck.

"Hey, Boss, we've got some bad news," yelled the guy they called Trasher.

"Tell me," the Boss said in a stern voice. He put down the free weights and walked toward the edge of the porch.

"Fucking dude must've come back while we looked for tools, man. Both lockers were open and stripped clean," said Trasher.

"You've got to be shitting me. How the fuck did you idiots allow that to happen? Let me guess, all four of you morons went looking for shit to open the lockers, and none of you geniuses stayed behind at the house in case he came back! Am I right?"

All of the men avoided his gaze. The Boss shone the flashlight on each one of them, scrutinizing their every move.

"Or did something else happen? Did one of you shit bags decide he was gonna get that treasure and cut the rest of us out of that shit? Seems too easy that there was nothing there. I think one of you is a liar," said the Boss.

He stepped down off the porch, quickly closing the distance between himself and the men.

"Really, Boss, we were all together looking for tools. None of us could have gone back to take anything," said Frankie, a slight tremble in his voice.

"No? Then you had help. Either way, one of you shits ripped me off," said the Boss.

Ortiz, a short Hispanic man with bad teeth and a lazy eye, started to say something, but Freddie wasn't in the mood for any more excuses. He pulled out the Glock he had stuffed in his waistband and pushed it into the side of Ortiz's head.

"Unless you gonna tell me what happened to the cop booty, I suggest you keep your piehole shut. You hear me, guaco?" said the Boss, shoving the gun into Ortiz's head so hard that the man stumbled backward.

"So if none of you dumb asses stole my stash, then where is it?"

"The dude who lives there, Charlie something or other, must have taken it. He probably showed up when we left. Maybe was even watching the joint while we were there doing our thing—you know all sneaky and cop like," said Trasher.

"So now I have two problems. No booty and a cop on the run."

"Yeah, Boss. Some sneaky shit he pulled on us. Must've really wanted whatever was in those lockers," Trasher offered hesitantly.

"You think? Here's what we're gonna do. Starting tomorrow, you boys are going to turn this entire town upside down. I don't care how many men it takes. I want every inch of this place turned over. And I mean every inch—and don't get lazy, include the attics and basements. This Charlie dude is either hiding in Porter or he ran. If he ran, I want to know where he ran to and who helped him," said the Boss. "He wasn't the only pig to skip town."

"You got it, Boss. We'll start on it first thing in the morning," said Trasher, signaling to the rest of the men to get moving.

The Boss watched the men climb back into the truck and drive off. Those four idiots represented the best men he could find in that PrisCorp hellhole. They weren't the brightest, but they were loyal to him, at least for now. The Boss knew that if something better came along, those loyalties would quickly shift.

— 31 —

Brown sat in the dark communications room of the Porter Police Department. The room was sweltering hot and the candle he used for light wasn't helping matters. In fact, it barely provided enough illumination for him to work the dials on the radio. Turning on the lights was not an option. He didn't want to draw anyone's attention to him. Brown knew the cops would talk again; at least he hoped they would. One way or the other, he needed to figure out their plan. He wanted to get ahead of this. If the cops were planning something against their Boss, he had to piece it together before it happened. If they were just sneaking cops out of town, with no other agenda, that could be useful information, too, especially if he could figure out where they were hiding. Several cops had escaped, posing a threat to the Boss.

Sitting in the dark quiet room, Brown began to think about the life he had before his life went south. His mind flashed to the look on his momma's face the first time she saw him in uniform. She'd looked at him like he was made of pure gold. Not the troubled shit he had been as a teenager and became once again after coming home. For once, his momma had been proud. He wished there was

123

some way to go back to that time. Maybe there was. Stretching his back and yawning, Brown looked at his watch, 12:40 a.m. He'd give it another hour before turning in for the night.

~ ~ ~

Charlie and Sam sat in front of the homemade radio. Charlie allowed Sam to fumble with the dials while he waited until Sam felt confident that their channel was dialed in as tightly as possible.

"Okay. Give it a try," said Sam.

"Marta, it's Charlie. You there?"

Static.

"Marta, you there?" repeated Charlie.

Static.

"Marta, come in. It's Charlie. Over," repeated Charlie.

Static.

"Maybe we're not broadcasting? We have power, but perhaps the antenna isn't working?" asked Charlie.

"It should be. I checked everything before we started. It all looks fine. Keep trying," suggested Sam.

"Marta, come in. It's Charlie. Over."

"Charlie? Is that you?" said Marta, her voice a faint echo through the static.

"Yes. It's me. I had to get out quickly this morning. I'm moving to HQ. I'll be in touch when we return. Tell the last one to sit tight. Over," said Charlie, chancing more than usual in their brief conversation.

"Will do. It sure is nice to hear your voice. Been worried over here. Over."

"Me too. Just sit tight. I'll be in touch when I have more info. Might be a few days."

"Okay, be careful out there."

"You too. Out."

Charlie put the speaker back on its cradle and rubbed his tired eyes.

~ ~ ~

Shit, here they go. It's that lady Marta again, thought Brown as he listened intently. He furiously moved the dials to enhance the sound quality, to no avail. There was more static than sound; however he heard enough to get the general gist of what they said.

After the conversation ended, Brown shut off the radio and closed up for the night. In the reflection of a dead computer monitor, he saw the door behind him to the communications room slowly open and then shut quickly. It was as though the person wanted to come in, but changed his mind once he saw Brown. He almost missed it.

Brown quickly and quietly blew out the candle and left the room. The station was deserted except for him and whoever had snuck in to use the radio. He had a strong suspicion he knew who had opened the door, but he wanted to confirm it without tipping his hand. Keeping a low profile while moving through the station, he glanced out the front windows. Brown saw Johnny walking quickly toward town. *Yep. That's what I thought.* He waited by the front door to the station until Johnny turned onto South Street and vanished. He opened the door as quietly as possible and sprinted toward the corner of Main and South. Tailing Johnny could be the key to everything.

Staying hidden behind bushes and trees, Brown was able to follow Johnny for several blocks. Finally, Johnny turned off the sidewalk onto a small walkway and disappeared behind a thick stand of bushes that blocked his view of a small covered porch. He heard a soft knocking from the porch and walked quietly through the adjacent yard to arrive next to massive bushes. Johnny knocked again and nothing happened. Brown waited impatiently, starting to wonder whether he was wasting his time. Johnny could be out doing any of a number of things.

When another round of soft raps on the door went unanswered, he considered skipping out ahead of the kid. If this was nothing, he didn't want to risk Johnny seeing him. All hope of quietly unraveling this little mystery would evaporate. They'd have to torture Johnny for the information or hold a gun to his grandma's head. Either way, Brown would lose control of the information and any benefit it could bring him. He shifted his weight, ready to leave, when the door cracked open.

"Marta, sorry to bother you, but it's urgent," said Johnny.

"Come in. Hurry before you're seen," said Marta, shutting the door after Johnny.

A sly smile crossed Brown's face. *What to do? What to do?* He now had a few options he didn't have a few minutes ago. He'd proceed carefully with his new discovery.

— 32 —

Sam quietly nestled into bed beside Jane. The warmth of her body made Sam long for her. For now he would be content to hold her while she slept. He buried his face into the back of her neck and breathed in the scent of her hair. Although Jane hadn't fully showered in a very long time, she still managed to smell faintly like flowers. He loved that about her.

"Did it work?" Jane asked sleepily.

"Yeah, go back to sleep," said Sam.

Jane turned to face him, breaking their embrace. "Why haven't you told anyone about the locker?"

"I guess it never came up."

"Come on. Really? The fact that we have a storage locker with a two-year supply of survival staples never came up?" said Jane.

"Well, you haven't offered anyone this bit of information, either," said Sam, stroking her face softly.

"Yeah, I'm really afraid. I'm afraid our supplies won't be there when we get home, at the house or storage unit. Who knows how long we'll need to be self-sustaining. I guess I just want to be sure we can manage on our own before I try to save others."

"I've thought about it all being gone, too. But it's pretty far out of the way, and people usually keep stuff they don't use in a storage locker. It wouldn't be high on my priority looting list."

"You have a looting list," she said, smiling.

"Yeah, and you're at the top of it, when all this is settled," said Sam, kissing her lips.

"I better be," she said, sighing. "I know you're right. Everything should be fine when we get there. I'm just being paranoid."

"A healthy dose of paranoia goes a long way. The real trick will be transporting the things we need to wherever we decide to hole up."

"I know it has been a while since I was in the locker, but don't we have bikes with pull-along carrier systems attached to them? We should be able to ride out with a lot of our supplies."

"We should be able to. But my concern is that these New Order guys are out there basically stealing food, water and everything else from people. We really don't want to be in a situation where we're caught on the road with supplies, and I'm not sure how useful the bike trailers will be on a rough trail," he said.

"We'll figure it out. Maybe the plan should be that we only travel at night. That way we'll have an easier time hiding."

"I think we'll need to do exactly that for part of the way. Maybe just while we get out of town. We can use the predawn hours to gain some distance from Evansville. I guess we'll have to wait and see what's happening in town. The situation there will determine our course of action," he said.

"What do you think is happening there? With Lea, I mean?"

"I don't know. So many scenarios run through my mind, some good ones, some not so good. Overall I have to believe that she's a smart kid who can take care of herself. I'm hoping it's enough…"

"Me too."

Neither Sam nor Jane wanted to dwell on their daughter's situation. There was nothing they could do from here, so they let the silence comfort them.

Jane kissed Sam passionately. "I love you more than you know. You always make me feel so safe and happy."

Laughing, Sam said, "Wait a minute, aren't you the police officer? You should be making me feel safe."

"Yeah, but it's always you who somehow does it for me."

"In more ways than one, I hope," said Sam before kissing her neck passionately in the dark.

"Yeah, in more ways than one…" said Jane, a little breathless.

— 33 —

Doris buzzed around her kitchen in the early predawn darkness, preparing packs of food for each of her guests to take with them. If her kitchen were fully operational, she would have baked some delicious snacks for them. In its current state, all she could offer was fresh fruits and vegetables, beans, nuts and hard-boiled eggs. She hoped it would be enough to help them reach their destinations. She was particularly concerned about Jenny. The poor child looked rail thin and exhausted. She seemed to eat nonstop since arriving at Doris's. Hopefully, the extra calories would help to put some meat on her little bones.

"Good morning, Doris. You're up early," said Charlie, rubbing his eyes.

"I thought I would send you all off with a nice farm breakfast. I have eggs and coffee cooking outside on the camp stove," she said.

"Are you using propane?"

"Sure am, why?" asked Doris.

"I don't want you to deplete your stockpile for us," said Charlie, sitting at the kitchen table.

"Nonsense. I have plenty of propane, and besides,

giving you all the strength to make it to the next house is the best use of what I have. I need you to make it back and start fighting for our towns. We all need it. Helping in this small way makes me feel like I'm doing my part."

"You are more than doing your part, Doris. Without your help we would never have been able to get as many officers and their families out of Porter. You've been a major part of the plan right from the beginning," said Charlie. "And if I may be so bold, I know your son would have been proud of you."

Doris stopped in her tracks and took a deep breath, her eyes moistening. "That might be the nicest thing anyone has said to me in a long time. Thank you."

"I don't think there's any question where your son got his bravery."

She nodded. "We all need to band together if we're going to defeat these New Order guys. Let me bring in the coffee. It should be ready."

Doris walked outside into the damp morning to fetch the coffee and eggs she had prepared. She stopped at the edge of the campfire and cried for a minute, hoping nobody noticed. Her role in righting this whole mess gave her the sense of purpose she'd lost with the death of her son. When she was composed, she wiped her face and returned with the campfire's bounty.

"Wow, that smells amazing," said Charlie, grabbing a steaming mug of fresh coffee.

"Please tell me I haven't been merely dreaming about the scent of fresh coffee," said Jane, walking into the kitchen with Sam close behind her.

"You're just in time. The coffee is fresh off the stove," said Doris, handing Sam and Jane aromatic mugs of coffee.

"Yumm…just what the doctor ordered—good coffee," said Jane.

"Hey, wait a minute. Haven't I been serving you the best camp coffee in the mountains for the last two weeks?" Sam said jokingly.

"Well—" said Jane to a round of laughter from Doris and Charlie.

"I also have eggs and a potato hash cooking. Everything should be ready shortly."

"You really amaze me, Doris. It seems like you haven't missed a beat during this entire crisis," said Sam, sipping his coffee.

Doris shared a quick look with Charlie, who smiled with pride.

"Well, being on a self-sustaining farm helps a lot. Over the years I have had my power outages. When you live way outside of town, the utility companies don't prioritize fixing the occasional power outage. After one particularly bad storm, I went for over two weeks with no electricity. An experience like that teaches you a lesson you don't forget. It's why I have two generators, a stockpile of chopped wood and plenty of gas and propane on hand to run just about everything."

"How did you manage to keep the fuel fresh? I assume you don't run the generators too often," asked Charlie.

"No, I really don't run them very often, but I have my farmhand rotate the gas into the various machines and purchase new fuel so that I always have a certain level. In the winter, I like to increase the amount on hand. You never know. It can be pretty isolated out here. Being prepared helps me feel calm about my circumstances, even being alone."

"Who knows how long the current outage will last. I'm

glad to know you'll be okay out here," said Sam.

"I should be just fine."

Returning to the kitchen, Doris brought in the perfectly cooked scrambled eggs and hash browns. She'd cooked the potatoes, onions and peppers in the fire the night before, giving them an unusual smoky flavor.

"Mind if we join you?" ask Mike.

"Not at all, please sit. Jenny, you can help me get a few more things to the table," said Doris, with a slight nod to Jenny. Jenny beamed at the invitation to help.

~ ~ ~

After breakfast, the group assembled their packs by the door in preparation to leave. Seeing the size of the stuffed packs always surprised Charlie. He often felt shocked by how much people carried on their backs, while simultaneously marveling at how little one actually needed on a daily basis. Moments like that made him think seriously about living in a tiny house, if he could squeeze a sixty-inch flat screen on one of the walls. If not, a slightly tiny house would have to do.

Pulling out the map and spreading it on the table, Charlie said, "Just so we're on the same page, the next safe house is here, and your home is here, correct?"

Jane and Sam nodded.

"You should plan to stay on the trail as long as you can. Or at least until this point," said Charlie, indicating the closest point of approach the trail made to their home.

"Do you really think the trail goes that far into Evansville?" asked Jane.

"I'm not entirely sure, because I've never been on it.

But people talk about taking extended camping and horseback riding trips that go from one end of the state to the other. I'm guessing you should be fine," said Charlie. "Just pay as close attention as possible to the trail. It could veer off considerably. When in doubt, take some time to determine your position and use your compass to go off trail."

"Yeah, we don't want a repeat of what happened when we tried to find your place," said Sam.

"Right. You have to assume you're in hostile territory at all times."

Sam grimaced. "Staying out of the town and its suburbs will likely give us the best chance of making it to Lea in one piece. After what we saw in Porter, I don't want to be anywhere near a populated area."

"You will have some urban areas to cross, right here," said Charlie, tracing a line on the map from the end of the trail to their house.

"It doesn't look too bad, maybe just a little over a mile. We could walk along the tree line and try to stay mostly hidden until this point," said Jane, pointing at the map.

"Yeah, you're right. We won't have a trail to follow, but might be able to pick our way through the trees and brush. I just hope one of our neighbors doesn't see us and call the police," said Sam, quickly blushing from his obvious mistake.

Everyone sat silent for a moment as his comment sank in.

Breaking the awkward silence, Charlie said, "From the distance on the map between your house and the next safe house, I think we might still be able to communicate with the handheld radios. The reception may not be good, but we should still be able to talk. I've set them all to the same channel. One we haven't used at any point so far. We should be able to talk without eavesdroppers, but keep all communications short on time and details, just in case."

"Okay, why don't we plan to touch base tonight. 12:30 a.m.? That way we can confirm everyone is safe," offered Jane.

"And just know that if things get out of hand, you can fall back to Scott's house if needed," said Charlie. "Just make sure nobody follows you there."

"You could also come back here," said Doris.

"Thank you, it really makes me feel better knowing that we have a place to come back to," said Jane.

"The company would do me good."

"I'm going to grab the last few things from the bedroom. We should be ready to go too," said Mike to Charlie.

"Sounds good."

"Jane, are you ready to roll?" asked Sam, tucking the map into his pants pocket.

"Sure am," said Jane.

Turning to Doris, Jane and Sam each hugged her and thanked her again for the much-needed rest and food.

"Charlie, we'll touch base tonight around 12:30 so long as everything goes okay," said Sam.

"I'll be listening for your call. Good luck. Remember, if you need help out there, don't hesitate to give me a shout. We're all in this together."

"Will do," said Sam, heaving his backpack onto his strong frame.

Charlie watched his friends make their way onto the horse trail. He worried for their safety. They hadn't experienced the full brunt of the New Order attacks on the towns. They had been tucked safely away in the mountains, enjoying a peaceful backpacking trip, when the murder and mayhem reached its peak. Living through the brutal New Order assault had awakened something in Charlie. He was now a man who would not hesitate, even for an instant, to defend himself and the people he was charged to protect.

Judging by the look on Jane's face when he'd shot the New Order man by the roadside, he knew she hadn't reached that point. She still operated under the old set of rules, which were no longer workable in this changed and dangerous world. Hesitation could spell the difference between life and death out there. The more he thought about it, the less convinced he was of their chances.

— 34 —

Marta lay in bed, trying to will herself up. The late nights waiting for Charlie to contact her were really starting to take their toll on her. To make matters worse, Johnny had stopped by unexpectedly last night, soon after she finished talking to Charlie. By the time Johnny left, Marta was so upset and scared from his news that she couldn't fall asleep despite her state of sheer exhaustion.

Johnny had told her that he thought a New Order man, a guy named Brown, overheard her conversation with Charlie. He said that she should not try to contact Charlie for at least a few days. Learning that the New Order might find her caused her to panic inside.

The obvious police rosters didn't include her name, which should buy her some time, but her paycheck was cut by the town of Porter. If this Brown guy heard her first name, he might be able to make a connection if he dug too deep into the paperwork files at the station. For the first time since the New Order's arrival, she felt completely exposed and vulnerable. If the New Order linked her to the communications, they would kill her in a particularly cruel manner. They were fond of torturing and killing anyone who helped the police, in order to make an example out of them.

Marta wanted to stay in bed until it all went away, but she knew that wasn't an option. Then again, she had no food to cook, no water to clean with and no job to go to. What was the point? Turning on her side and nestling under the covers, she heard a disturbance outside.

"You've already taken everything from us! We have nothing left!" shouted her neighbor Jim Hunt.

"Shut the fuck up and open the goddamned door, or I'll blow your fucking head off. You still have that, don't you?" said Tico to a round of laughter from his New Order buddies.

Hearing the exchange, Marta froze in place. *What's going on now?* Padding over to the bedroom window, she cautiously moved the curtain aside and peered out. New Order men were everywhere, on foot and in vehicles. It appeared that they were going door-to-door, searching or stealing again. Raids had become a common occurrence of the past two weeks. First, the New Order had stolen all useful items and food from the residents of Porter. Then they'd begun searching "for pigs," as they put it. The occasional discovery of an officer in hiding bolstered their confidence and resulted in more searches.

Oh shit. What if they're looking for the mystery radio user? They could be going door-to-door to find whoever is communicating with the cops.

Panic, followed by a nauseating adrenaline rush, hit her hard and fast. Quickly shrugging on shorts and a T-shirt, she ran to the attic, taking the steps two at a time. The radio must be hidden as fast as possible; her life depended on it. Just as she made it into the hot, dark attic, a loud banging on her front door rang through the house, sending a shockwave of fear through her body.

She quickly threw a tarp over the radio. The tarp would not be enough to hide the radio, but it was the only thing she could do quickly. The angry banging on the door grew in intensity. Either she would have to open it, or the door would be kicked in. She quickly climbed out of the attic, shutting the door behind her.

"Yes, can I help you?" Marta said to the tall New Order man at her doorstep.

"I'm coming in to search. Now!" shouted the man as he shoved her aside and barged into the house.

"Close the door quick. We don't have much time!" shouted the man.

"What are you talking—"

"Just do it!" he shouted.

Marta hesitantly closed the heavy wooden door. She was reluctant to be alone with any man, but being alone with a convicted felon terrified her.

"Listen, my name is Brown. I am or was a resident of PrisCorp until all of this went down," said Brown. "I need to go along with these guys or I will be killed. Do you understand?"

Through her fear, all Marta could manage by way of a reply was a simple head nod.

"I know you worked for the cops and have been using a radio to communicate with them. I also know that you're probably responsible for getting a lot of cops out of here," said Brown.

Marta's legs trembled uncontrollably, and she began to sweat profusely. She felt the world spinning around her and started to black out.

"You there, lady?" said Brown, shaking her.

That was the last thing she heard before finding herself lying on the couch, her vision returning.

"For shit's sake. You with me again?" asked Brown.

"Y-yes," she said groggily.

"I don't have a lot of time before some of the others might try to get into your house. I know you work with the cops. When the shit hits the fan and the cops make their move, I want to help them. I can't be on the New Order side. I want you to tell them that."

"Why would you do that?" was all Marta managed to say through her swirling thoughts.

"Because the cops always win. Those idiots think they can keep living here like kings. They're all one stupider than the other. Eventually, the cops or the military will take back the town. I just want to serve my time and move on with life. I've made some mistakes in my life—I don't want to make another."

Feeling a little better, Marta said, "Who else knows about the radio?

"No one as far as I know. I was a radioman in the Navy and hung out in the comms room at the station because it was safe for me in there. It also gave me something to do that didn't involve murder and rape. The guys mostly thought it was a waste of time, and so did I until last night when I heard you talking to that guy Charlie. I pieced the rest together and here I am. Look, lady, I have no reason to support those assholes. I didn't gang bang inside and I don't intend to now. I just need to survive," said Brown.

"Why are they searching? What are they looking for?" asked Marta.

"Somehow those idiots figured out where your friend Charlie lived. They raided the place, but couldn't get into his gun lockers. They left his house to get tools, and when they returned with the tools, the lockers were emptied.

The Boss is shit-fire mad about it. He wants Charlie found and skinned alive as an example."

"Jesus."

"Yeah. Charlie needs to stay away from town. I have to go now before they get suspicious. If I hear anything else, I'll let you know. In the meantime, don't answer the door," said Brown with urgency.

Brown got up and left Marta's home with a soft closing of the door. Outside, she heard him talking to some other New Order guys.

"Searched this shithole top to bottom, ain't nothing in there. Let's move on," said Brown to two New Order men as they approached the house.

Marta couldn't stop shaking. The surprise of what Brown had told her made her worry for Charlie and Johnny. She somehow needed to warn both of them. She wanted to trust Brown, but the events of the last two weeks had taught her that trust was hard earned.

— 35 —

Jane and Sam followed the horse trail north, snaking their way through dense forest and some open areas, just as Charlie thought it would. They reached a few points along the journey where the trail split or veered off significantly, and Sam had to make a choice based on his compass and the knowledge he'd gained over the past two weeks.

"Do you really think Doris will be okay out there alone?" said Jane, breaking their silence.

"I think she should be fine. She makes most dedicated preppers look bad," said Sam.

"I'm not talking about her supplies. Do you think she'll be safe from the New Order?" said Jane, with an obvious edge in her voice.

"I knew what you meant. I'm just trying to lighten the mood a little. You've been off all morning?"

"I'm so worried about what we'll find when we get home. The closer we get, the worse I feel. It should be the opposite."

"I know. Me too," said Sam as he squeezed her hand.

The obvious marking of the trail seemed to thin out, leaving Sam with that nervous feeling again.

"Hey, let's stop for a minute. I need to get my bearings. We should be getting close to our break-off point. If that's the case, we need to make it to the tree line so we can start working our way through the back of the neighborhood."

"Can you believe we've lived here so long and never knew about this trail?"

"Actually, I can. We always seem to leave for trips, hiking included. It never occurred to me to look right in our backyard. Besides, this is more like a trespassing excursion. I think we've violated the property rights of dozens of people on this little walk of ours," said Sam.

Sam laid the map on the ground and considered it for a moment. Jane tapped his shoulder. When he looked up at her, she was pointing toward the trees behind him.

"I think that's the Reynolds' house!" she whispered.

He turned on his knees and stared through the forest, catching a glimpse of the telltale dark blue siding. "So much for looking at the map. I guess I should have just opened my eyes. I guess we could start here and work our way through the development to our house."

"Do you smell that?" asked Jane.

"The smoke?"

"Yeah. It's really bad."

"I noticed it a while back, but didn't want to say anything. It's been getting stronger."

Breaking out of the tree line closer to their house, Jane and Sam discovered the charred remains of several houses. Half of the street in front of them had completely burned to the ground. Peering through the standing houses, they could see numerous other houses burned down as well. Smoke gently rose from the charred bones of several houses.

"Shit. What happened here?" said Jane, staring into the distance.

"Hey, hey…Jane, Sam! Over here!" called a lone male voice.

A familiar man stood on his back patio, waving his arms and motioning for them to join him.

"Who is that again? I don't remember his name," said Jane.

"I think it's Mike. No wait. It's Mark. He's the guy who moved in a few years ago from somewhere out west. I think he's widowed, with no kids. Does some sort of computer work. We met him at the fall neighborhood party."

"Okay. Right. I remember him. Nice guy, from what I recall," said Jane. "Do you think it's safe?"

"I don't know, but it's too late to hide. If they're using Mark as bait, they know we're here."

"I guess you're right. Stay on your toes," said Jane.

"Yep."

They approached Mark, who looked a little hesitant to leave his patio. Beyond that, he didn't sense anything off with Mark's behavior.

"Hey, Mark," said Sam.

Mark was unshaven and filthy, and his eyes darted across the landscape of the backyard. He appeared to be anxiously searching for something.

"Hurry up. Come inside before they see you," said Mark, ushering them in through the open sliding glass door into his kitchen.

The house sat completely dark and still. Mark had closed all the blinds and taped every shade to its window frame, ensuring no one could look inside, even at an angle. The kitchen island, table and countertops were coated in a fine white layer of dust, same as the hardwood floor. Footprints trailed off in every direction. The rest of the house looked like it had been turned over in a tornado. Things were strewn across the floor. Tables and chairs sat on their sides. Sam wondered why Mark chose to leave the house like this.

More worrisome, a sickly metallic odor permeated the rooms, assaulting his senses. He knew the smell immediately. Blood. Glancing at Jane, Sam tried to assess whether she'd smelled it too. The worried look on her face suggested she had.

"It's good to see you guys. I've been alone here for the past couple of weeks. Too afraid to go outside much," said Mark. "Where did you come from? I thought you lived in the other direction."

"We were out on a backcountry hiking trip. When we walked out of the mountains, we came back to all of this," said Sam.

"Whatever this is," added Jane.

"Well, you missed everything, thankfully. The power went out probably shortly after you left—then all hell broke loose," said Mark.

"We walked here from the north entrance to the park. We passed through Porter. An escaped gang from PrisCorp took over the town. It's a real mess out there. They call themselves the New Order. Have you seen anything like that here?" asked Jane, hoping he hadn't.

"Unfortunately, I'm well acquainted with this New Order. They rolled through and ransacked the houses. They stole anything of value and trashed the properties, leaving them useless to the homeowners. Then they started the fires. They basically burned down the house of anyone who resisted. The fire department is gone, obviously, so once they started a fire, it just sort of kept going to the next house along the line until it finally died out on its own."

"Shit. It almost sounds worse than in Porter. Those guys didn't start any fires," said Sam. "What about the people?"

"Most people fled. I stayed awake at night, watching the dots of flashlights moving through the neighborhood. They all seemed to walk north. Not sure where they were going. I haven't heard that things were better in other areas, so I stayed put, figuring the New Order already got what they wanted here."

"What is that god-awful smell? Sorry to insult you, Mark, but it reeks in here," said Jane.

"Yeah, it is pretty strong with the windows all closed up. I have a deer hanging in the garage. They stole all of my food, not that I would have had any left by this point anyway," said Mark with a shrug. "I've been hunting in the woods. Yesterday, I snagged a deer with my crossbow. At least I managed to keep that hidden from the dummies. I had to wait until nighttime to drag it back and hang it up. I'm hoping they don't come back and discover the deer. So far, they haven't detected my presence. I left the downstairs like it is and taped the window shades tight. My hope is that I ride this thing out until the cops come back."

"I'm not sure you recall, but Jane is with the Evansville PD," said Sam.

"Sorry, Jane. I completely forgot. Where is everyone? Why aren't the police out rounding up those guys?" asked Mark.

"The Porter and Evansville PDs were caught off guard by the PrisCorp gangs. Close to eight hundred of them strolled out of the facility. They quickly overpowered the Porter PD and started hunting down officers. The Evansville PD managed to get most of the police out of town ahead of the mob. They didn't want to leave, but there's nothing they could have done against hundreds of armed thugs. The departments are now working together to take the towns back. You said most of the neighbors are gone, why did you stay?" asked Jane.

"I have nowhere to go. This is my home. New Order or not. The living has been hard, but I'm managing.

"It doesn't look like you've been staying here. Where are you living?" asked Jane, glancing around the still home.

"Come on. I'll show you."

Mark led them upstairs into a small, sparsely furnished spare bedroom. Reaching toward the ceiling, he grabbed a concealed notch between the ceiling and the crown molding. With one slight pull, a hidden staircase slowly lowered itself into the room.

"Holy smokes. Nice!" said Sam, clearly appreciating the mechanical genius that went into building the cleverly concealed staircase. The staircase's existence was so well hidden that one would never realize it was there unless they saw it come down. Mark had created the perfect hiding spot.

"Thanks. I made the stairs a while ago, almost right after moving in. I planned to use the attic for storing computer equipment. Expensive stuff I don't want lying around in my home office. I never ended up doing anything with it. I've been hiding up there ever since."

"You said 'searching as usual.' What did you mean by that? Do they search often?" asked Jane.

"They would barge into the house almost daily at first.

I think they expected people were hiding things. Other times, I think they were either bored or just trying to intimidate us. They took everyone's guns, knives and anything else that could be used as a weapon. It was terrifying. Things have settled down a bit, but I still wouldn't recommend turning on a light of any kind. It seems to draw them in like moths."

The attic ran the entire length of the house. The steep roofline gave the space a high ceiling in the middle, with sloping sides, making it impossible to stand close to the front or back of the house. A table, mattress with blankets and stacks of clothing sat against one of the darkened windows. Empty cans of food, a camp cook stove and water containers were strewn across the floor several feet away. On the opposite side of the house, he spied a covered bucket in the corner. He assumed the very strong human waste odor came from the bucket. Mark must have read his mind.

"Yeah. The bucket is very nasty. But there's no sewer service. I have to use the bucket and pour the waste out in the woods. It isn't great, but it has been working."

"It's actually a really good idea. Looks like you attached it to a lever by the window to lower it down?" said Sam, once again admiring Mark's ingenuity.

"Yeah. The last thing I need is to be sloshing shit water around my house, not that it would make much of a difference at this point. Eventually I hope to move back downstairs. Whenever that might be," said Mark with a shrug.

"I'm not sure you recall, but we live on the other side of the development. We left our daughter, Lea, alone at the house. We haven't been in contact with her since we left. Have you seen or heard anything about her?" asked Jane.

"No, I haven't talked to anyone. I kept my head down from the beginning."

"That's fine. You did the right thing. These people sound ruthless. I guess we'll find out all we need to know once we get there," said Jane.

Sam took this as their cue to get moving.

"We need to get going. We hope to grab our daughter and head out of town," said Sam. "You're more than welcome to join us on the way out. We know a safe place, where you don't have to hide in the attic and crap in a bucket."

"Let me think about it," said Mark.

"Don't take too long," said Jane. "If all goes according to plan, we should be back through here in less than an hour."

"Fair enough. Your house is on the north side of the neighborhood, right?" asked Mark.

"Yeah, why?" asked Jane.

"You need to figure out the best way to get there unseen. Some of the New Order guys moved into a house on that side," said Mark, pointing to the north-facing window.

"Good idea. Are they just in the one house?" asked Jane.

"I have no idea. My view is somewhat limited, but I've been trying to figure out where they are so I can work around them. I'm getting concerned about my water supply. At night I've been reconning the surrounding areas, searching for ways to get water and fuel. I got lucky with the fuel, but I'm still trying to find a plentiful water source," said Mark.

149

"Recon? Were you on active duty?" asked Sam.

"A long time ago. Well, not that long ago. I served my enlistment in the Marine infantry, spending some time in Battalion Recon. I stayed in the reserves for a while after I left Camp Lejeune. Made staff sergeant, but got too busy with travel at work to stay in the active reserves. You?"

"Fleet Marine Force corpsman. Made petty officer, second class, before I came to my senses," returned Sam with a slight smile.

"Small world," said Mark.

"Do you mind if I pull back the shade a bit to scan the neighborhood," said Jane, crouched at the window.

"Just a crack should be fine," said Mark.

"Shit. There are cars parked at our house," said Jane.

Sam raced to the window, placing his head next to Jane's. The front lawn of their house was crowded with two pickup trucks and a small beat-up sedan. A black, 1970s-era Trans Am sat in their driveway. He knew that Trans Am all too well. He'd dreamed about lighting it on fire, along with its owner, more times than he cared to admit. Their worst nightmare had come true. Tank was back, and he was with the New Order.

"We need to get over there. Fast," said Sam, heading toward the stairs.

"Your house is the one with the cars on the lawn?" asked Mark, an alarmed look on his face.

"Yeah. Our daughter is still there. We have to go. Now," said Jane.

"You can't just walk into that house. The New Order guys have been living there—almost from the start," said Mark.

"Let's go. Maybe we can reason with them. Get Lea

and leave. They can have everything," said Sam, taking the first step on the homemade stairs.

"Hold on, you guys. You can't just barge in there and reason with them. They'll kill the two of you on the spot," said Mark. "Think this through. It has been over two weeks. Your daughter might have left with one of the neighbors before everything started going to shit. She could be anywhere, and yes, she could still be in the house. The only way you'll get her away from those jackals is by force, which you might be able to pull off with your load out. But you need to make sure she's there before you go storming the doors," said Mark. "Would be an awful waste to bust in there and find out she's gone."

"He's right. We need to stop and think this out. We've come too far to blow it now," said Jane.

"Here's what I'd do," said Mark, pointing out the window. "See that white house on the left? I haven't seen anyone there the whole time. I think your neighbors must have been gone when all this went down and never made it back," said Mark. You sit tight there and gather some intel before you do anything. You have to think through every move you're gonna make, inside and outside. One knocked-over chair, a flash from a light—anything can put an end to your mission."

"That's the Cramers' house. I think they were in Kentucky for their annual family visit. Everything must've happened while they were away, like us," said Jane.

"Alright. We break into their house and watch our home for any signs of Lea. Maybe we'll get lucky and see her. Who knows, maybe she and Tank rekindled something and he's treating her well," said Sam.

"You're kidding, right?" said Jane, with an incredulous look.

"Just being hopeful," said Sam. "I hate to think of the alternative."

"Who's this Tank character?" asked Mark.

"He's our daughter's ex-boyfriend. Six foot two, two hundred and fifty pounds, with a shaved head and prominent neck tattoos," said Jane.

"Aryan Brotherhood?"

"He's been known to hang with them," said Jane.

"A real charmer," said Sam.

"I bet. I've seen him in action. It's hard not to. He's everywhere. Your boy, Tank, is in charge of this area. He's their chief asshole or whatever he calls himself. He's one mean son of a bitch. I watched him assassinate a few of our neighbors for no reason at all. Be careful with him," warned Mark.

"We really don't have a choice," said Sam.

"Use the tree line for cover. Then cut in through there, between the yellow and tan houses. If you need any help at all, close the shades in the corner room of the Cramers' second floor. I'll see it and get to you as quick as I can," said Mark.

"Thanks, man. You've been really helpful. Hopefully, we'll be able to return the favor," said Sam, shaking Mark's hand.

"Seriously, be careful out there. Those guys will kill you on sight—or worse."

— 36 —

Breaking in to the back door of the Cramers' garage was not as difficult or as loud as Jane thought it might be. Sam lightly cracked a pane of glass in the door and carefully pried one of the larger pieces of glass out with his folding knife. Once the piece was removed, he pulled the rest out and unlocked the door.

Like Mark's house, the Cramers' house looked disheveled and picked over. The pantry doors stood open and the refrigerator was picked clean of anything useful. The bedroom closets were open, clothing tossed throughout the rooms.

"Geez, you would think those guys could've left the kid's room alone," said Jane.

"Yeah, it does seem really senseless to trash a little girl's room. Good thing the Cramers weren't home. I'd hate to think what Tank and his crew would do to children."

"They're absolute garbage. We need to get Lea and get out of here as soon as possible," said Jane.

The master bedroom afforded them a perfect view of the front of their home. Sam took out his binoculars and stood far enough away from the window to remain hidden.

"Let's see what we have."

"Given that there are four vehicles parked in our yard and driveway, we can assume that there are at least four of them in there," said Jane.

"Maybe. Maybe not. I'm not making any assumptions with Lea's life on the line. Right now, I only care about seeing one person—Lea. Maybe I'll get lucky and see her standing close to a window."

"I doubt it. We might have to get in there and search," said Jane.

"I was really hoping you wouldn't suggest that. I don't like our odds."

"I don't see how we have a choice," stated Jane.

"I know. Maybe we'll see an obvious opening or some kind of pattern in their behavior we can use. We might be able to get in and get out quickly," said Sam.

"We can only hope. You keep watching. I'm going to look around to see if I can find anything we might need. I don't think Stacy or Jim would mind."

"I don't think you're going to find much," said Sam. "Those animals took everything."

~ ~ ~

Lea Archer's head pounded from dehydration and malnourishment. Sitting alone in her family's basement, she'd lost track of the days. Time seemed to pass in a blur of either abject boredom or sheer panic. At times, it felt to her that her confinement in the basement had just begun. At other times, she feared she had been chained to the metal support beam for weeks. In either case, she'd all but lost hope that she would be rescued either by her parents or anyone else.

The days following the power outage were terrifying. Without the constant hum of electricity-fueled machines, the world became eerily silent, until faceless strangers started to scream in the night. Blinded by a deep darkness, she had no way to discern the location of the screaming or the nature of it. Night after night, bloodcurdling shrieks punctuated the silence, creating a complete state of panic for Lea.

Her parents probably had no idea of the danger she faced. In the beginning she kept a calendar of the days, carefully marking time until they would walk out of the mountains and arrive back home. She knew they would have no reason to leave the mountains early, and when they did, it would take them a few more days to walk back. The thought of being alone for that long terrified her.

A couple of days after the lights went out, the sound of a lone vehicle rumbled through the neighborhood. Lea knew it was Tank's Trans Am within seconds. Her first instinct was fear. They'd broken up several months ago, after she suffered a year and a half of constant emotional and physical abuse at his hands.

He'd been all right at first, but his true colors shone shortly after they started dating and partying together. It took her far too long to overcome his iron fist and walk out of the relationship. Actually, she hadn't exactly walked out. She'd been driven to a recovery center by her parents. Somewhere Tank couldn't find her. Lea hadn't seen him since she got back, most likely due to her mom being a police officer and her dad promising to kill him if he ever showed up again.

When Tank drove his Trans Am up the driveway like nothing happened after the power failed, she'd been rightfully scared. She should have trusted that instinct and hidden herself or ran out the back door. Instead, she almost welcomed him, for the perceived safety he represented against the chaos unfolding outside the house. He could be charming and frighteningly sincere sounding when he wanted to be. If she had only known that Tank was the one responsible for the insanity.

"I came to make sure you're okay. You are the only person in the world that matters to me. I want to make up for everything between us and make sure you're safe. I want to be with you and protect you."

He looked kind, thoughtful, and even a little sweet. She unbolted the door and wrapped her arms around his thick neck, allowing his strong, heavily muscled arms to encircle her. For the first time since the incident, she felt safe.

A day or so after Tank moved in, he left to get supplies. He returned with more food, candles, flashlights and booze than she would have thought possible. She was a little worried about the alcohol, given that she had been dry since arriving at the recovery center and wanted to keep it that way.

When she asked him how he had acquired so much stuff, he bashed her across the face with the back of his hand and shouted that she should mind her own fucking business. The real Tank was back. He'd actually never left. The beatings slowly increased to an almost predictable daily affair. At first she tried everything she could to avoid making him angry, but nothing worked. Every time he came back from town, he would punch, kick or simply slap her. Her face and body were covered in bruises and welts that never disappeared. She was sure her nose had been broken and one of her front teeth had been knocked out.

The beatings got so severe, she knew it was just a matter of time before he killed her. Determined to survive, Lea quickly packed a bag of essentials and planned to leave while he was in town. Moving around the house, collecting anything she could use to survive, along with some sentimental things, kept her busy. On the day she planned to leave, her pack sat near the door while she filled her last water canteen. Suddenly she heard the sound of Tank's Trans Am grinding through the neighborhood. Panic hit her hard. She moved through the house, trying to conceal the last efforts of preparation for leaving. Thinking she'd covered her tracks, she flopped down on the couch and waited for him to come through the front door.

As usual, he stormed into the house, intending to beat her after he pounded down some cheap booze. That was the pattern. Go out. Return. Start drinking. Beat Lea. While in the kitchen rummaging for a bottle, he suddenly stopped moving. Silence filled the house. The sound of her heart pounding loudly in her head drowned out the sound of her breathing and panicked thoughts. In her haste to conceal the evidence of her imminent departure, she'd merely shoved her backpack into the kitchen pantry. The pack's size and heft made it impossible to put back into the basement before he came into the house. He hadn't been gone long, so she'd hoped he would be in and out of the house quickly and the pack would go unnoticed.

Bursting through the kitchen door into the family room, Tank screamed, "*You fucking bitch! You planned to leave me! After everything I've done for you!"* His fists rained down on her in an animalistic fury. Blow after blow, she struggled to hold on to herself, shielding her face as best she could from his rage. The last thing she recalled seeing was the metal toe of Tank's now bloody work boot—just before he rammed it into her broken nose.

She woke in the basement, tied to the metal support beam, the lower half of her body slumped against the cold concrete. Her arms and shoulders ached from their static position around the beam. Waves of unbearable hunger and thirst punched through the pain. From her new prison, she heard voices upstairs day and night and knew Tank had moved several men into the house. She worked on the rope ties that bound her, trying to loosen them—but knowing it was futile.

— 37 —

Jane crouched below the window of the Cramers' master bedroom. Frustration clawed at her while she surveyed her home for signs of Lea. Hours had passed without seeing her. From Jane's vantage point, she could determine that five men had taken residence in her home. She'd angrily watched Tank and four other men take turns urinating in her side yard flower garden—wanting nothing more than to drill a bullet through each of their skulls. Continued restraint observing these animals got more difficult as the hours passed. Jane now freely fantasized about bursting through the front door with a baseball bat and bashing their heads in, one by one. Of course, she knew her fantasy would never come to pass. But visualizing her triumph over Tank and his crew was strangely soothing.

Walking into the bedroom, Sam asked, "Any sign of her?"

"No. Just Tank and his four buddies pissing all over my flowers."

"Sorry, you did work really hard on that garden. For what it's worth, it looked great when we left."

159

"I'm beginning to wonder if Mark was right. Maybe Lea has left and we're just waiting around for nothing. It's clear that they made the yard their toilet. If Lea were there, I would think she would've needed to relieve herself by now. But there has been no sign of her. I'm really starting to wonder if she is gone."

"The thought crossed my mind too, but we can't leave until we look through the house," he said.

"Yeah, I need to see for myself. I would like to see some of her stuff missing—like her hiking boots, sunglasses and purse. Anything. Then I'd know she made it out. But where would she go? How will we ever find her?"

"I don't know. All I do know is that we need to wait and keep watching the house. As soon as we see an opening, we run over there and search as quickly as we can. After that, we get out of Evansville. With or without her."

"She might've heard the force is gathering in the northeast. Maybe if she isn't there, she's heading to the new HQ—looking for us."

"We can only hope. Besides, if she is gone, she has supplies at her disposal, right? She knows about the storage unit. I would imagine she would go there first to gear up."

"I think you're assuming she listened to all of our survival talk. Let's face it, most of what we say goes in one ear, out the other," said Jane. "She certainly didn't listen to us about Tank, and we could see that problem coming a mile away."

"Yeah, you're probably right about that. One step at a time," said Sam. "If she's not in the house, we'll figure something out."

160

Turning her gaze back to her home, Jane sat quietly scanning each window with binoculars. As time passed, surveillance of their home became increasingly difficult. With night falling, darkness blanketed the neighborhood. Jane knew not much more would be gained by looking out into the darkness. However, she could not pull herself away. Watching for Lea made her feel like she was actually doing something for their daughter. Still holding out hope that she was alive.

Neither of them had wanted to bring up the possibility that she hadn't survived the past two weeks. That they might find their daughter in the house—dead. She didn't want to think about it.

"You hungry? I have some of the granola Doris gave us, along with peaches and some nuts," said Sam.

She turned her gaze away from the house.

"I didn't notice before, but now that you brought up food, I'm starving. Where should we go to eat? We really can't put on any flashlights in here, or they might see us. Remember what Mark said about the light drawing Tank and his guys into homes?"

"Right. I checked out the basement earlier, and it's nicely furnished. The finished part of the basement has no windows. I don't see any reason we can't use flashlights down there."

Jane took a last look through the window, willing Lea to step out of the shadows. Only a vast, empty darkness returned her long stare.

Jane and Sam moved carefully through the pitch-black house, using the house's predictable floorplan as their only guide. Once through the kitchen and on the basement stairs, the hand railing allowed them to walk confidently down into the home's subterranean level.

"Hold on. I'm going to close the door and jam some socks under it. That way none of the light we use down here will escape the basement," said Sam, busying himself at the door.

"Good choice. Not only will the light be kept from leaving the basement, but the stench of those socks will ward off any would-be intruders."

"Thanks, I aim to please," said Sam.

Turning on the flashlight, Jane said, "That's better. I'm glad you did some exploring. I've been so fixated on Lea that I didn't even consider where we would sleep or how we would get around in the dark."

"Yeah, I was thinking about how dark it was at Charlie's and Doris's houses, even with candles and flashlights. After what Mark said, I figured we needed a spot to land that didn't allow any light to escape."

"Speaking of Charlie, I'm going to try to contact him in a couple of hours. They should be at the next safe house if all went as planned."

"Sounds like a plan. It'll be nice to hear they got there in one piece. I know the two safe houses are fairly close, but given what we encountered on the horse trail, I'm starting to think anything can happen out there."

"Did you catch what Mark said about everyone moving north?" asked Jane.

"Yeah, I've been thinking about that a lot. I sort of had a rough plan that we would get Lea, resupply at the storage unit and then walk or ride bikes north—maybe to the lake. I figured we could occupy one of the summer cottages," said Sam.

"I thought the same thing, though I'm sure we're not the only ones who came up with that plan. If enough people took off in that direction, who knows? There might not be room left for us up there."

"All we can do is focus on the first part of the plan—finding Lea," said Sam, shaking a few peanuts from a bag.

~ ~ ~

The night was the worst for Lea. The basement was dark and dingy enough during the day, but when the sun began to set, pitch darkness enveloped her quickly. Alone, sitting on the cement floor with her hands bound to the metal pole in front of her, she was terrified of the night. Her mind searched the darkness for familiar sounds. Any unusual noises started an uncontrollable cascade of horrific mental images. She pictured spiders, rats, mice, even snakes were coming to get her, crawling across her skin, into her ears, tangled in her hair. She begged Tank to let her out, just during the night. His typical response: *"You should thank me for not killing you, you dumb bitch."* He always punctuated his responses with a swift kick to her bruised side or stomach. At this point, she'd rather deal with the unknown in the dark than Tank. She often wondered if death would be merciful compared to the miserable fate that undoubtedly awaited her.

When her wish for death started to become a fixation, she would try to recall the History Channel shows she'd watched with her dad about POWs. They were trained to keep fighting and resisting, even in captivity, when their situation was the grimmest. They continuously searched for ways to escape or foil the enemy's plans. Recalling their struggles and triumphs gave Lea the strength she needed to continue to fight against Tank. There wasn't much she could do, but she wasn't ready to give up, so she did the best she could.

Lea worked on the ropes that held her to the metal support post at night. Tank never came into the basement in the dark, so she rubbed the ropes back and forth across the pole, trying to create enough heat and friction to fray her bindings and break free. She knew it would take a while, but she had nothing but time at this point.

When she got careless, her charm bracelet would clang against the metal pole. It wasn't a loud sound, but it stopped her cold, especially during the late evening and early morning hours, when the house was still. She'd wait for Tank to burst through the doors. He rarely checked her ropes closely enough or with any regularity to notice the fraying. She would use his laziness against him. Lea determined to keep working against Tank until the ropes finally broke and she could sneak out in search of her parents.

She'd long ago given up hope that her parents would return to the neighborhood.

~ ~ ~

Sitting on the floor in one of the bedrooms facing the back of the house, Jane held the radio under the window. The handheld had a limited range, so they hoped to give their signal the best chance of reaching Charlie at the next safe house.

"Did he give us extra batteries for this?" she said, radio in hand.

"Yeah, he gave us a whole bunch, but considering the radio is our only means of communication, we should use it sparingly," said Sam.

"Alright. I'll give it a few tries. Maybe we'll get lucky," she said, pressing the transmit button.

The orange glow from the radio's LED display cast a dim light in the room. She took her thumb off the button, worried that the light might give them away.

"Damn thing is bright," she said.

"I totally spaced out on that—should have known better," replied Sam. "I think we're fine as long as nobody's out for a walk in the woods, but I'll lower the shades to make sure."

Jane waited for her husband to finish with the blinds before trying again.

"Charlie...it's Jane. You there? Charlie? It's Jane. Over."

Static filled the bedroom.

"Charlie? Hello? It's Jane."

"Maybe we should give it a little while and try again? It's not quite midnight. He said to contact him between 12:00 a.m. and 12:30 a.m.," said Sam.

"Okay, but I'll leave it on in case he calls us first."

They lay together on the single bed, holding each other while listening to the crickets and other insects they rarely heard during the summer months. They spent most of the summer holed up inside the house, windows shut and the central air conditioner working overtime to keep the heat and humidity at bay. The thought of air-conditioning reminded her that the house was stifling. Regardless of how sticky she felt, it was good to have Sam's arms wrapped around her. Leaning against each other in the dark, taking in the stillness outside, Jane felt like they were the only people in this changed world.

After about fifteen minutes, she started to seriously overheat, sweat dripping onto the pillow.

"I'll try again," she said, looking for an excuse to get up.

"Charlie, you there? Over."

Nothing.

"Charlie, it's Jane. Over."

Empty static answered her call. At 12:40 a.m. Sam took the radio out of Jane's hand and turned it off. Pulling her closer to him, he said, "I know what you're thinking, and they're probably fine. It's the distance. I wasn't very confident we'd be able to reach them from here."

"Thanks for saying that. I needed to hear it, even if I don't believe it," said Jane as she leaned into him—sweat be damned.

— 38 —

Charlie and Mike sat on the floor in Scott Marsh's family room. The soft sound of Jenny's deep, rhythmic breathing filled the otherwise silent room. If only they could all sleep so easily. Unfortunately, they weren't out of the woods by a long shot. The Marshes' situation underscored the problem presumably faced by everyone in the county—possibly the state or country. A problem that was on the verge of becoming a significant threat to everyone's survival. The Marshes had very little in the way of essential supplies.

The Marshes' house had been chosen as one of the safe houses because of its location along the route to the consolidated headquarters, with little regard to their meager and seriously depleted supply situation. Charlie shared all of the food and water Doris supplied them with, leaving the Marshes extremely grateful. It was the least they could do for a family that had taken on such an important role with no organized logistical support from the police.

They had become noticeably gaunter since the last time Charlie had seen them. Seeing their condition, he suggested that they visit Doris. He knew Doris would be more than willing to resupply them. Although Barbara seemed willing, even excited to go to Doris's house, Scott wouldn't budge. He couldn't tell if fear or pride drove the decision, and it didn't matter. In order to survive, he'd have to get over it and make the trip to Doris's. The route was safe enough, though he couldn't blame Scott for worrying about the outside world. After what Charlie had seen, he wouldn't blame anyone for staying put.

"You should try it again. One more time," said Mike.

"Jane…you there? It's Charlie. Jane?"

More static. Charlie had already tried several times, with no success.

"It's useless. They're probably out of range. I thought we would be close enough, but I guess I was wrong," said Charlie.

"Or something happened," said Mike.

"Or that, which is all the more reason to stop trying to contact them. If something did happened to Jane and Sam, whoever is on the other end could be listening to us. Last thing we need is one of the New Order guys actively looking for whomever is on the other end of the radio."

"I know you're right, but I feel bad just sitting here comfortably knowing they could be in danger," said Mike.

"I'll leave for their house before sunup and check on the situation. I should be able to get there around mid to late morning. If anything, I can confirm they're fine, then come back here to take you and Jenny the rest of the way to headquarters," said Charlie.

"I'll go with you. No way am I letting you go there on your own."

"I appreciate the offer, but you need to stay here and keep Jenny calm. She needs to rest or we'll never make it to the HQ. Once we leave here, we'll travel across some heavily populated areas. We'll need to be more agile, moving as fast as possible, responding to or avoiding threats as they arise. Right now, Jenny is exhausted. She could barely make it here—and it was an easy stroll along the horse trail," said Charlie.

"I know you're right, but it just sucks to send you out there alone, especially with Jane and Sam potentially in trouble."

"I plan to make my way into the neighborhood and watch their house from a distance. I'll just get a look at what's happening from a safe vantage point. If they are in trouble, we can work up a plan to go back and rescue them."

"Deal," said Mike.

— 39 —

Early the next morning, before the sun rose, Jane resumed her post in the master bedroom window. Things appeared calm across the street. Jane assumed the guys were all still sleeping, because none of them had materialized in the side yard to urinate. Again, Jane's mind turned dark as she fantasized about shooting each man as he relieved himself on her flowers.

"Anything yet?" asked Sam as he walked into the bedroom.

"No. I don't think they're up yet. No one has come out to pee."

"Do you think they leave at all during the day? Where would they go?"

"I'm guessing they leave. Probably to steal stuff from somewhere else. Whatever our neighbors didn't take north has obviously been stolen. Plus, you'd think they'd go crazy from the boredom. These idiots need constant entertainment. Without television or video games, I suspect they'll take off at some point."

As Jane said the words, her mind flashed images of Lea being used as "entertainment" by five men. Seeing the look on Sam's face, she was sure he had considered the same thing. She needed Sam to be a rock for her—and Lea. She quickly changed the subject before either of them started talking about it.

"How about a snack while we wait? I'm sure they're just sleeping off their hangovers. Once cottonmouth and the need to pee starts breaking through the hangover fog, they'll start piling out. We'll get our chance to search the house. Part of me thinks we should just shoot them as they come outside. One by one."

"You mean assassinate them in cold blood?" said Sam.

"Yes—that is exactly what I'm suggesting. I don't see how this is going down without someone dying. I would rather they die," said Jane, with a fierce look in her eye.

"I absolutely agree. I have no problem killing each and every one of those lunatics, but we need to determine if Lea is inside before we start shooting. If she's in there, we can't take the chance of screwing up the ambush. They could use her as a human shield and take off with her. Then what? First we find her. If we can't sneak her out, we'll come up with a plan."

A few minutes later, the short, skinny guy walked out the back door and pissed on Jane's flowerpots.

"Really? You had to hit the pots too? Isn't it enough that you all ruined my beds?" complained Jane.

Tank and each of the other four men rotated in and out of the yard throughout the morning to relieve themselves. As the hours ticked by, Jane began to wonder if they were wrong about the guys leaving. Other than the predictable rotation into the yard, there were no real signs that the entire group would ever leave the house. Maybe she would get to shoot one of them pissing on her flowers.

"How long do you think we should wait? Maybe we

need to create a diversion that will draw all of them out? Then one of us can sneak in to search while they're out of the house," said Jane.

"Not yet. Let's give it at least a full day. If we still haven't been able to get inside the house by the end of the day, we can talk to Mark and see if he's willing to help us create some sort of diversion," said Sam.

"That's a lot to ask of Mark, and I'm not sure what he can do for us with a crossbow."

"He is a Marine. I suspect he would be willing to help. Besides, he has way more at his disposal than a crossbow."

"What do you mean?"

"While the two of you were crouched at the window, looking at our house, I happened to notice the tip of a gun sticking out from under a blanket. Given the size of the mass concealed by the blanket, my guess is that Mark is sitting on quite the arsenal."

"Interesting. Maybe he built the third-floor storage access to hide more than just sensitive computer equipment."

"That would be my guess—" started Sam.

Before he could finish his sentence, the side door to their home across the street burst open with a loud bang. All five men scrambled out of the house in a jumbled rush. Tank and one man hopped into the Trans Am while the other three loaded into the pickup truck. The two vehicles roared out of the driveway and raced past the Cramers' house, heading out of the neighborhood.

"Here's our chance. Let's go!" said Sam, grabbing his rifle.

Jane snagged her rifle and ran with Sam through the Cramers' house, desperate to find their daughter.

~ ~ ~

The sound of the back door slamming shut roused Lea from a light sleep. Hearing the door slam, she assumed the guys had left for the day, as they often did. Sitting quietly, straining to listen to the noises in the house, Lea waited to be sure they were all gone before she furiously sawed at the ropes.

One time, Lea had thought they were gone, but didn't realize Tank sat quietly alone upstairs. The sound of her bracelet tapping against the metal pole drew him into the basement. He untied her and yanked her to her feet by her hair, ripping out a large clump in the process. Once she was standing, he punched her in the stomach so hard that she flew across the room, bashing her head and back against the furnace. This time, she would be more careful.

After a few minutes of listening intently for the slightest movement upstairs, Lea began to work on the ropes with all her strength and concentration. If she could just get a little more to fray, she might be able to pull the rest of the rope strands away with her teeth. The back door creaked open slowly, gently closing. That asshole was trying to trick her! Not happening. She sat perfectly still and waited.

~ ~ ~

Charlie worked his way through Jane's neighborhood, carefully moving between the remains of burnt houses. He could hardly believe the New Order had nearly burned the neighborhood to the ground. Knowing Jane's street address but not the layout of the neighborhood made his progress slower than he would have liked. He hoped to get to her house, check in and make it back to Scott's before dark. At this rate, he was not sure he would make it.

Finally, he spotted their street sign through his binoculars and calculated that the house should be about midway down the street. He started to work his way through the bushes and trees separating the lots, concealing his approach as best as possible from observation in all directions. When he was one house away, he decided to hide in the wild grasses behind the next-door neighbor's home and watch Jane's house from a safe distance. Surveillance was warranted in a situation like this. He wanted to be sure he did not walk into a trap.

After settling into place, Charlie watched as five men took turns whizzing on Jane's flowers. There was no sign of either Sam or Jane. The men looked to be New Order types, heavily tattooed and unkempt. Charlie knew there was no way either Jane or Sam was in their house with these men. He also suspected that if they had already been caught, he might see evidence of their demise. The neighborhood's streets were marked by frequent splatters or long smears of dried blood, but nothing to indicate a recent execution.

When the men piled out of the Archers' house and drove away at full speed, Charlie considered investigating the house before returning to the safe house. Before he could lift himself from the ground, Jane and Sam crossed the street, running toward their house. In an instant, he knew exactly what they were doing, searching for Lea. He started to rise, but thought better of it. If either of them saw movement, they might open fire and accidentally kill him. Charlie stayed low, waiting for the right time to call out their names—but they vanished into the house before he could say anything.

He determined to stay put and offer them over-watch protection. From his position, he could cover the driveway and the approaching street. If the New Order returned, he would be ready for them.

— 40 —

Walking through the side door of their house, Sam didn't feel like it was home anymore. He glanced at Jane to determine if she felt it too. The look of anger on her face confirmed that she felt the same way. The house had been stained by these foul beasts, and no amount of physical repair or cleaning could set that right again.

Dishes sat piled high in the sink and all over the counter. The pantry shelves were picked clean, the garbage overflowed, and dried spills covered the counters and floor. A strong slightly sweet smell of rotting garbage clung to Sam's nose as he ventured further into the house.

"We should start upstairs and move as quickly as possible," whispered Jane.

"Okay, let's stay together. Who knows, there could be another guy tucked away in this mess. I don't want any surprises."

"Me neither," said Jane, aiming her rifle up the stairway and leading them slowly up.

The bedrooms and bathrooms looked exactly as Sam expected. The New Order guys didn't discriminate between their partying zone and sleeping areas. Both were equally disgusting. A huge fist-sized hole greeted them at the top of the stairs, adjacent to the closed bathroom door. With Jane covering the bedroom hallway with her weapon, Sam quietly opened the door and pushed it in several inches. The moment the bathroom came into view, he wished he'd kept the door shut.

A deep brown sludge overflowed down the edges of the toilet, the stench nearly causing him to gag. Flies buzzed angrily around the bowl, undisturbed by his entry. Broken glass from the shattered bathroom mirror littered the sink basin and floor. He leaned as far in as he could tolerate to check the bathtub for Lea. They had to be thorough. Alive or dead, if she was in this house, they had to know. Based on what he'd seen so far, he couldn't imagine she was alive—if she'd been here when Tank arrived. His head reached a point inside where he could see enough of the bathtub to determine that she wasn't lying in the feces-filled tub.

Jane glanced over her shoulder when he closed the door, looking for some kind of answer. He winked at her, indicating that it was all right. His wife edged forward, easing into place next to Lea's door. Sam leaned against the opposite side of the hallway, covering the other bedroom doors.

"Lea?" whispered Jane into Lea's room. "Lea?"

They waited, listening for movement. When nothing stirred, Jane entered her room, followed by Sam, who stood guard at the door. Over his shoulder, he saw the same mess as they'd left throughout the rest of the house. Wrappers. Beer cans. Cigarette butts. On closer inspection, her room appeared to have suffered the most damage that they'd seen so far.

Evidence of rage clung to the walls, unnerving Sam. It appeared that someone had kicked two holes in the wall near Lea's bed. Sam feared the worst for his only child. Seeing her childhood room in this condition broke Sam's heart—and stoked his rage.

"I'm going to kill every last one of them," whispered Sam.

"We'll worry about that later. Look around for her stuff. If she managed to leave, she would have taken her phone and purse at the very least—even without power, she's addicted to that phone. Sunglasses, too. I'm not sure what else, but I know she never leaves home without those. We should check for her hiking boots or running shoes downstairs," suggested Jane as she searched Lea's room.

"I don't see anything that she normally uses. Even her favorite hairbrush is gone."

"I know. And there's nothing downstairs to indicate she's still living here."

"Let's check the other bedrooms and downstairs again. Maybe we missed something."

The remaining bedrooms held no clues about Lea's fate—just more trash and human waste. They carefully made their way back down the stairs and looked around for anything they might have missed. Sam searched the landing area next to the kitchen for Lea's shoes. He found her running shoes, but her hiking boots were gone. All signs pointed to the likelihood that she'd bolted north with the neighbors when it became apparent that things would get out of control in Evansville. He hoped she was safe, wherever she'd landed.

"Her hiking boots are gone," he said. "We have to assume she's gone."

Holding the door open, Jane nodded.

"We should go. We'll have to rethink our plan. Maybe head north."

"That's what I'm thinking. Let me just check the medicine cabinet before we take off. Maybe we'll get lucky and some of our medications will still be there," said Sam, disappearing into the hallway off the family room.

"Okay. Just hurry," said Jane, letting the door shut.

Sam stuffed his cargo pockets with the few remaining bottles of over-the-counter medicines he could find in the bathroom mirror cabinet. All of the prescription-strength painkillers, sleeping pills and muscle relaxants were gone.

~ ~ ~

Hearing the kitchen door close, Lea worked on the ropes again, her bracelet chiming rhythmically against the metal beam. *Come on. Just a little more.*

Lea knew she might not have a lot of time before they piled back into the house. If she managed to break through the ropes this time, she could grab her backpack and run. Tank had thrown it in the corner of the basement when he dragged her down into her personal dungeon. The bag mocked her—too far away to reach, but close enough to obsess over. In a way, it also gave her hope. When she broke free, she had everything she needed to escape in one place. The idiot hadn't bothered to search the bag to find the power bars and water filtration pump she'd packed.

~ ~ ~

"Did you hear that?" asked Jane, stepping carefully into the kitchen.

Sam shook his head before crouching with his rifle aimed toward the front of the house. She held her index finger to her lips, and they settled into absolute silence. Listening intently, Jane heard the faint sound again. It was a high-pitched, rhythmic—possibly metal-on-metal sound.

"That!" she whispered excitedly.

"What is it?"

"I don't know. But it sounds like it's coming from the basement. We never checked the basement!"

"Damn. We almost skipped it," said Sam.

"You keep an eye on the street," she said. "I'll check it out. Lea might be down there."

"Jane, her stuff is missing—including her backpack."

"We have to look," she said before slowly twisting the doorknob on the basement door.

She carefully opened the door to the basement and eased quietly onto the first stair. The sound stopped. Jane's thumb pressed against the pressure switch on the rifle's vertical grip, ready to activate the light. She softly moved down each stair, mindful of her steps in the darkness, until she reached the concrete floor.

As her natural night vision improved, the dim outline of a human form slumped on the floor started to materialize. Before Jane could take a step forward, the figure started to feverishly move its hands against the metal support beam.

"No. No," the woman whimpered.

She could tell it was a woman. Her thumb triggered the powerful rifle light, illuminating the space and concentrating a bright beam on a dirty, disheveled young woman. Horror and relief washed over Jane. She'd found their daughter.

"Lea! Oh my God!"

"Mom?" said Lea.

Tears streamed down Jane's face as she ran to her child. She laid the rifle on the floor and took out a flashlight, turning it on. She nestled next to her daughter and kissed her filthy forehead.

"Mom!" Lea sobbed into her shoulder, unable to move more than a few inches toward Jane.

"We have to get you out of here. Are you okay? Can you walk? Are you injured?"

"I think I can walk. I haven't stood up in a while. Just get me out of here. They could be coming back! They always do!"

"Lea!" yelled Sam, bursting into the basement. "You're here! My God, we almost left!"

Sam hugged her tightly before standing up and digging through one of his pockets.

"We need to cut the ropes and get the hell out of here, fast," said Sam.

Jane clung to Lea despite her awkward sitting position and the overwhelming fecal stench. Clearly, Lea had been held in the basement for a long time with no regard for her cleanliness or health. A fierce anger arose in Jane. Thoughts of revenge washed through her mind as she hugged Lea and stroked her greasy hair.

"We'll get you out of here. We have a safe place for all of us."

Sam cursed, pounding the support beam with his fist. "Damn it! This knife isn't good enough. The rope is wound tightly around her wrists, and it's some kind of super-durable material. Like a towrope. I just can't get through it with my utility knife without getting really sloppy. I need the hunting knife from my pack. I'll run back to the house to grab it."

"No! Daddy, don't go!" screamed Lea.

Standing in front of her, Sam said, "Maybe I have something in the garage that can cut through this more easily. I'll be right back."

Jane sat on the floor, holding Lea to comfort her. Intense love and relief filled Jane, obliterating her immediate thoughts of revenge. Her sole focus was getting Lea out of the house and as far away from Evansville as possible. Glancing at the ropes around Lea's wrists, she realized what Sam meant about the ropes being tied too tightly. They had wrapped the thick ropes around so many times that cutting into the coils would require a very sharp knife and a skillful hand. Otherwise, Lea's wrists could get sliced in the process. Turning her gaze to the steps, Jane waited for Sam.

— 41 —

Mark Jordan sat in front of his attic window, watching the neighborhood through the slit in his curtains. His daily ritual was more meaningful now that Jane and Sam were out there, looking for their daughter. He kept a careful watch over the Cramers' house; particularly the bedroom window they agreed would be their point of communication. So far, they had not indicated a need for help.

He had to hand it to Jane and Sam. They'd kept a low profile at the Cramers' house, creating absolutely no obvious indications that they occupied the home. He did not see the telltale sweeping of flashlights or any other visible sign of their occupancy. Things had been so quiet over there that Mark began to wonder if they had already left the development. If they had, he hoped they had found their daughter alive, taking her with them.

Peering through his spotting scope, he saw the side door fly open. As usual, the New Order men piled out of the house and drove off, screeching tires as they raced out of the neighborhood. The pattern of their daily departure was hard to predict, but they almost always left at some point and usually in a hurry. He figured the New Order had some kind of communications network, possibly alerting them to the discovery of hidden civilians or a cache of supplies. Gunshots often followed their departure.

The wildcard was their return. Some days they were gone until almost dark. Other days they would be out and back in less than an hour, sooner in some cases. He often wondered where they went and what kind of horrible things they inflicted on innocent people in other parts of the town. The end of New Order's occupancy couldn't come fast enough. Hearing from Jane that the police had a plan to push back into the town gave Mark hope.

Mark's trained eyes caught movement in the Cramers' yard. Jane and Sam moved quickly across the street from the side of the Cramers' house, weapons ready. They paused briefly at the side of their house before disappearing through the side door.

Shit. He nervously looked at the entrance to the neighborhood. The New Order men could come back at any moment. He'd witnessed a few false starts when they returned a few minutes later to grab something they'd forgotten. He wondered if Jane and Sam knew how precarious their situation might be. If captured, they might be executed on the spot, like some of the other neighbors.

He'd have to be their eyes and ears. There was only one way in or out of the neighborhood using the roads, so he'd spot them early enough. He just wasn't sure what he could do to warn Jane and Sam. Shifting his eyes back and forth between Jane's house and the entrance to the neighborhood, Mark decided to unveil a little surprise he'd hoped to find an excuse to use.

Mark stepped away from the window and pulled a green blanket off the small arsenal he kept ready for any occasion. A compact, AR-15-style rifle with a red dot optical sight lay on its side, magazine inserted. A longer, similar-looking rifle with a sizable scope rested on an extended bipod next to it. He kneeled to grab the longer rifle and a few spare rifle magazines before returning to the windowsill.

He'd purchased the specialized rifle a year after getting out of the Marine Corps, hoping to keep his basic sniper skills intact. The weapon was a civilian version of the Squad Advanced Marksman Rifle (SAM-R) he had carried in Force Recon. Essentially, it was a tricked-out model of the M-16A4, with a slightly heavier barrel and precision trigger.

Mark set the bipod feet on the inside windowsill molding and sighted in on the Cramers' house for reference. No screen stood in the way, because Mark anticipated the possible need to shoot out of the window and had previously removed the screens. The scope was set at its maximum magnification, which gave him a reasonable field of view at this distance. Just as he settled into the folding chair beneath him, Mark detected movement from the road leading to their neighborhood.

Damn it, guys. You need to get out of there. Having already chambered a round for ready use, he disengaged the safety and centered the crosshairs on the turn into the neighborhood. Sure enough, he caught sight of both cars heading back toward the Archers' house. The Trans Am was first, followed closely by the pickup truck.

He had no way to easily warn Jane and Sam. There certainly wasn't enough time for him to run to their house. Instead, he needed to create a diversion to alert

Jane while simultaneously slowing down the New Order's approach.

Mark made a few quick mental calculations, following the convoy through the scope as the vehicles bored deeper into the neighborhood. He centered the crosshairs on the Trans Am, deciding whether to shoot the driver, passenger or tires. He chose the tires, in the hope that they would not know what hit them. Perhaps the driver would guess they had a tire blowout?

He waited until the Trans Am moved closer. Closer. And finally the cars headed straight down the street, lined up with his window. An easy shot, if there was such a thing. *Wait for it. Wait for it. Slow and steady.* Mark exhaled and applied even pressure to the trigger, sending a single bullet through the calm neighborhood.

The bullet hit the bumper of the Trans Am, just to the left of the front driver's side tire. *Shit.* Quickly readjusting the crosshairs, he eased the trigger back again, hoping the sound of the muscle car's engine drowned out the distant gunfire. The rifle kicked, and by the time he found the cars in the scope again, the tire was flopping in its wheel well. Direct hit.

The car veered back and forth across the street as the driver tried to overcorrect. Tires and metal squealed as the car braked, feet from crashing into a disabled SUV parked on the right side of the road. The driver, who Mark assumed to be Tank, repeatedly kicked the tire and punched the hood of his car.

Shifting his scope back to the Archers' house, Mark waited for any sign that Jane and Sam had heard the warning shot and escaped. If necessary, Mark wouldn't hesitate to shoot the men if they got too close to the house. Meeting Jane and Sam earlier had shifted something inside Mark. He'd no longer sit by and allow innocent people to be massacred. He'd once again take the fight to the enemy. One bullet at a time.

— 42 —

Jane watched Sam's desperate effort to cut the ropes. Sam had come back from searching the garage crestfallen. The New Order men had been through the garage, making a mess and stealing their tools. The small utility knife he wore on his belt turned out to be the best blade he could find, and Jane knew it would not be enough. Sam needed his razor-sharp hunting knife.

"This isn't working," she said. "I think you need to get your hunting knife."

"I'm not leaving you here," said Sam.

"We don't have a choice," said Jane, cocking her head to the side. "Did you hear that?"

"What?" asked Sam as he carefully worked on the reinforced rope.

"Gunshot. We need to hurry. I'll run upstairs and see if I can figure out what's happening out there," said Jane, moving from Lea.

"No! Don't leave me!" screamed Lea.

"It's okay. I'm not leaving you. I just need to get upstairs. We need to be sure no one is coming. Dad just needs a little more time to work on the ropes."

Jane glanced at Sam, hoping for a silent cue as to how

long he thought it would take. Sam shook his head almost imperceptibly; he could not cut the ropes with the pitiful knives at his disposal. The best he could do was try.

She grabbed her rifle and ran upstairs, taking two steps at a time. Scrambling to the front windows, she peeked out into the neighborhood. Tank's Trans Am was stalled five houses away, a gaggle of men standing in a semicircle around the hood. Tank gestured emphatically, slapping one of them on the back of his bald head before pointing at the Archers' house. The man nodded and turned toward her. Jane raced back to the basement.

"Sam, we have to go, now! There's no more time! They're coming back. We need to leave now!" yelled Jane, running into the basement.

"No! You can't. They'll kill me. Please! Don't go!" Lea shouted hysterically.

Jane placed her hands on Lea's cheeks and pulled her face close. "We're staying at the Cramers', keeping a close watch on the house. We are not leaving you. We would never leave. Right now, we have to go back and get better tools to cut this rope. I need you to be strong for me. Just a little longer and we will get you out. Just a little longer. Can you do that for me?"

Interrupting her, Lea said, "The ropes are almost cut through. See? I've been working on it and I'm almost through!"

Lea moved her hands back and forth furiously. The charm bracelet chimed against the pole with her harried movements. "See?"

The rope showed little sign of wear. Lea's efforts would have never freed her. The only thing Lea had accomplished so far was to rub the skin on her wrists raw. She was delusional.

"Okay, baby. You keep working on that, quietly. We're right across the street. One way or the other, we will get you out of here. Just hang on a little longer," said Sam, pulling a pill bottle out of his pocket. "Take this. It'll help." He handed her a small white pill.

Lea grabbed it and swallowed hard.

"You'll be fine. Just a little while and we will be back. Promise," said Jane through tears.

Leaving Lea in the basement was the hardest thing Jane had ever done. Knowing that her child sat in her own excrement, helpless and brutalized, hardened Jane to their current situation. Jane's determination to take revenge on Tank and the other men reached a fever pitch as they sprinted across their backyard to the cover of a thick stand of bushes.

— 43 —

Mark watched as two New Order men ran toward Jane's house, presumably intent on retrieving a spare tire. Suddenly, the side door flew open. Sam and Jane ran out the side door and toward the cover of bushes behind the next-door neighbor's house. He knew, as they did, that they could not cross the street without being spotted. They needed to take cover immediately and wait until it was clear to move again.

Just as they moved toward the neighbor's house, Mark caught sight of a man hiding in the high grass at the back of the neighbor's lot, holding a military-style rifle. Mark knew Jane and Sam could not see the concealed man as they ran from their home. Instead, they were running almost directly into him. The man didn't look like a New Order type, but that didn't mean anything in these changed times. Neither Sam nor Jane had mentioned a traveling companion. The man hiding might be a New Order assassin just waiting to take his shot.

Mark positioned the crosshairs on the man's head and started to apply pressure to the trigger. Before his index finger broke the trigger, the man stood up and started emphatically waving both hands in the air, directing Sam and Jane to a safe hiding spot. Mark engaged the safety and removed his finger from the trigger well, his hand shaking. He'd almost killed an innocent man.

~ ~ ~

"Jane! Over here!" said a familiar voice.

She scanned the neighbor's backyard, seeing Charlie rise from the grass at the back of the yard. He waved his hands and arms.

"Get over here fast! They'll see you!"

Sam grabbed her hand and pulled her across the yard. They both dove into the grass next to Charlie, who lowered himself slowly, keeping his rifle aimed back at the Archers' house.

"Charlie? Geez, what are you doing here?" whispered Jane.

"Saving your asses, obviously," said Charlie.

"Nice," she replied.

"I heard two gunshots. No idea where they came from," said Charlie.

"Two? I only heard one," said Jane. "Our daughter is in there. She's alive, but they have her tied to a pole in the basement. We couldn't get her out before they came back. We need to get back inside. Can you cover us?" asked Jane excitedly.

"Against all five of them?" whispered Charlie as gruff voices cut across the backyard.

"Jane, I need something heavier to cut her free. They used a heavy-duty towrope. We need a better plan. Shooting them as they walk may or may not work. We need to be certain. We can't chance a botched shoot-out. If one of them gets back into the house—then what?"

Sam's words slowly sank through the fog of adrenaline that clouded Jane's thoughts. She knew he was right, but all she could think of doing was shooting the men on the street as they walked smugly back to their house. Sam's words rang true. They needed to be certain that all the men were neutralized; otherwise Lea could be killed.

"You're right. Damn it. We're so close. To leave her like that, it's just not right," said Jane, choking back tears.

"Not to sound insensitive, but if your daughter survived this long, she'll make it a few more hours. We need to get off the streets and into a safe place before we can do anything. Where are you guys holed up?" asked Charlie.

"Across the street, the white house on the right," said Sam.

"Alright. We need to wait until dark before we can get back there. We can't chance crossing the street. Let's back up into the thicker brush and hunker down for a while. If they all leave again, we'll be in the perfect position to try again," said Charlie before unsheathing a wicked-looking knife. "I think this will cut through those ropes."

"I think you're right," said Sam.

The three friends crawled to a more concealed location in the yard and waited for darkness. Jane's mind kept returning to Lea, hopeful for the first time in weeks despite the rage that consumed her.

— 44 —

After the crew discovered Charlie's house, the Boss turned all of his attention toward finding the cops' escape route. He seemed to take Charlie's removal of his guns personally, demonstrating a single-minded focus on finding and killing everyone that assisted the police.

The Boss assigned Brown and a guy named Cherry to drive out of town in search of Paul Reed and Jack Reilly. The pair never returned from a routine patrol, and he wanted both men returned—dead or alive. Brown knew firsthand that if he found them alive, they'd expire shortly after the Boss got his hands on them. Reed and Reilly were as good as dead, no matter what was up with them.

Brown assumed that the two had fueled up their Chevy Impala and driven out of town, hoping to escape. They wouldn't be the first, or the last. As the days droned on, dozens of men deserted the Boss and his murderous mission, seeing life under him as nothing more than a new form of imprisonment.

The small army he had led to Porter had started to dwindle down to true believers, as Brown privately thought of them. The true believers were those that sided with the Boss on every one of his cruel, harebrained schemes, never questioning their orders. Whether they were cruel by nature or simply too afraid to leave didn't really matter. They were one and the same, and despite the continued desertions, the true believers numbered close to fifty men. More than enough to spread their reign of terror to several towns.

As he drove around with Cherry, Brown gave some serious thought to skipping out on the madness; however, he couldn't be certain where Cherry's loyalties fell. Cherry never showed the Boss the kind of extreme loyalty that got him rewarded with women and extra booze, like many of the other men had, but he hadn't shown any overt signs of growing weary with the Boss's antics. A quick eye roll here or subtle head shake there spoke volumes about a man's true feelings. Cherry had kept a poker face from the beginning, giving Brown nothing to work with when determining Cherry's loyalties.

Brown knew that even suggesting to the wrong person that he wanted to leave was a death sentence. No. He'd keep driving Cherry around until sunset, without mentioning his plans to help the cops. At sunset, the two could return to the Boss and report that the search failed to find either Reed or Reilly. Brown also considered that the smartest option might be to stab Cherry in the neck and put as much distance between himself and Porter as possible. The Boss was becoming less rational by the hour.

As the day dragged on, Brown's mind started to drift as far away from his present reality as possible. He'd long ago passed his limit of tolerating Cherry's stupid commentary about everything they passed on the road. The man couldn't shut the hell up. He was seriously considering the throat-stabbing option when something metallic in the forest reflected light. He hoped Cherry didn't see it.

"Did you see that?" asked Cherry.

Of course Cherry had seen it. The guy never missed anything, or an opportunity to talk about it.

"You're starting to see things," said Brown.

Investigating the source of the reflection was something Brown wanted to avoid. Not only did he want to finish off the shift without delay, he was worried that the cops were hiding a vehicle or something in the trees.

"You need to stop, man! There's something hidden back there—off the side of the road. Shit, it could be Reed and Reilly! Those assholes might be trying to hide out or something, or they crashed off the road."

"Alright, don't get your panties in a twist," said Brown, seeing no way around it.

Brown slowly turned the car around and drove back to the approximate point where they'd both seen something in the woods. Cherry got out of the car first, apparently anxious to discover something the Boss would be grateful to learn. Seeing Cherry's excitement made Brown very relieved that he'd kept his mouth shut about his own plans.

"Check this out! I see tire tracks in the grass. Looks like a car drove into the woods."

The two followed the faint tracks into the woods. Not far off the road, they discovered the Chevy Impala, previously driven by Reed and Reilly, nestled between two trees. Branches haphazardly scattered across the vehicle had mostly concealed it from the road.

"Shit! This is the car they were driving! Looks like those assholes just left it here. If they were leaving, they'd be way better off driving. Right? Why the fuck would they want to walk?" asked Cherry.

"How the hell should I know? Those two weren't exactly the brightest guys I ever met. Maybe they thought walking gave them a better chance to hide? Come on, let's get out of here."

"I'll just have a look in the car. Maybe I can drive it back. The Boss will be happy if we at least return the car."

"Can't argue with that," said Brown, feigning interest in the scene.

Cherry walked over to the driver's side door, peering through the windows as he approached. Just as he stretched his hand out to open the door, he froze, staring at the side of the car.

"Check for the keys so we can get out of here. I don't want to be stuck out here after dark," said Brown.

"Check this out," said Cherry, pointing to the door.

"What is it?"

"Looks like dried blood," said Cherry, kneeling down to get a closer look.

"It's probably mud."

"Don't look like mud to me."

Brown pushed his way through the brush and headed to Cherry. On the way over, he noticed a trampled path leading to the right. No point in drawing Cherry's attention to it. He got the distinct impression that they had stumbled on the work of a resistance group. A group smart enough to know that they couldn't drive a car around without drawing the wrong kind of attention.

He crouched next to Cherry to take a look at the car. A coating of brownish-red droplets covered a section of the driver's side window and door. It appeared to be a very fine mist of dried blood. Brown scraped his nail against the substance and tasted it—spitting immediately.

"Definitely blood," said Brown, unable to get the metallic taste out of his mouth.

"What do you think happened?"

"Beats me. If I had to guess, I'd say they turned on each other," said Brown, eyeing Cherry cautiously.

"Maybe we should search around a little more."

"Aren't you gonna check for the keys?"

"Oh yeah," said Cherry.

Brown walked back to the second path as Cherry dug through the car. He used his feet to move some of the brush to try to camouflage the trampled foliage. There wasn't much he could do without bending over and using his hands, so he stood where the trail started, hoping Cherry would pass him without noticing.

"I don't see shit in here!" said Cherry. "One of them must have taken the keys."

"Let's get out of here. One of them might be watching us from a distance—planning to pick us off."

His statement had a chilling effect on Cherry. The man crouched, peering into the woods around him. *Now he's going all tactical? What a dumb shit.* Cherry walked quietly and deliberately back to Brown, a look of fear in his eyes.

"We should have brought one of the rifles out of the car," whispered Cherry.

"Good point. We should remember that next time," said Brown. "Let's head back and report this to the Boss."

"No argument there," said Cherry, scanning the forest again.

He squinted past Brown. "Move over," said Cherry, nudging past him.

So much for hiding the trail. Brown just hoped he'd scared

Cherry enough to dissuade him from exploring any further.

"Looks like another trail. All flattened out like they dragged something into the woods. We need to check this out," hissed Cherry.

"With one of those traitors out there? There's no way I'm going deeper into those woods without an army."

"And there's no way you ain't," said Cherry, pointing his pistol at Brown.

"Shit. You don't have to threaten me," said Brown, slightly raising his hands. "Let's get this over with and get the hell out of here."

They found a body several yards into the forest. The man looked peaceful, almost like he was sleeping, a small hole in his head the only indication it was a permanent nap.

"Satisfied? We found the body we both knew would be here. Now, let's go. It's obvious that they fought and Reed took off."

Cherry searched the body, finding nothing.

"Yeah, unless something else happened to them. It just doesn't make sense. If Reed did split, he would have been better off taking the car, not leaving it here and taking the keys."

Glancing around the forest, Cherry started to move through the brush deeper into the forest.

"Where are you going?"

"I'm going to check it out. I think I see something a little ways into the forest," he said, stopping in his tracks. "Look!"

A second body lay on the forest floor, a gaping wound in the center of the man's chest. The man appeared to have died where he was shot.

"Holy shit. They were ambushed! Wait until the Boss hears about this! What's that over there? Is that a jar?"

An unbroken mason jar sat in stark contrast to its surroundings, suggesting the existence of others. Cherry picked up the jar and inspected it closely, sniffing the inside of it. "It smells like peaches."

Brown knew they must have stumbled on the trail that the cops used to get people out of town. He needed to make sure Cherry did not put things together.

"Peaches? You must be hungry. Let's get back to town. We can tell the Boss we found them and the car," suggested Brown.

"Look over there—it's a trail! Holy shit! This is it! We discovered the trail the cops are using to get people out of town! Wait until the Boss hears this! Fucking cops must've killed Reed and Reilly, then hid the car!" Cherry said excitedly.

"You want to keep your damn mouth shut?" said Brown. "They might still be out here."

"Damn. You're right. We need to report this immediately," said Cherry. "We found how they're sneaking some of the cops out."

"How can you be so sure? We have no idea what went down here. Two bodies and a jar don't equal some kind of underground railroad."

"It ain't no railroad. It's a trail," said Cherry.

"That's just a term for a hidden trail," said Brown, amazed that Cherry was dumber than he looked.

"Whatever you call it, that's what it is," he whispered excitedly. "The trail runs parallel to the road. The road runs directly north, out of town. Reed and Reilly must've stumbled on the cops and got themselves killed."

"I don't know, seems like a stretch. Besides, I don't

want to give the Boss bad intel. He'll go ape-shit crazy if we're wrong," said Brown, desperate to get Cherry off the idea.

The thought of giving the Boss incorrect intel seemed to slow Cherry down. Brown could see the seeds of doubt starting to bloom behind Cherry's cold stupid eyes. Being wrong would get both of them killed. Clearly, Cherry wanted to rise in the Boss's ranks, not get killed.

"To find the start of the trail, all we need to do is follow the road back to town. The trailhead has to be close by the road," said Cherry.

"If you say so, man. I just don't want to take any heat if we're wrong," said Brown, trying once again to dissuade him.

Cherry was right. They'd found the trail leading out of town. It would be only a matter of time before the Boss had every available guy on the trail, looking for runners and the people harboring them. Eventually, they'd find what they were looking for. Brown knew he needed to warn Marta, fast.

— 45 —

Safely in the basement of the Cramers' house, Sam couldn't sit still. He paced the small space, trying to relieve the tension, anger and anticipation. Seeing his baby girl being held in such deplorable conditions drove him mad. All he could think about was getting her back, no matter what the cost. Somehow he had managed to pull Jane back from the brink of disaster in their neighbor's backyard. If the same decision had been put to him now, he'd vote for charging in—guns blazing.

For the first time in his life, Sam had trouble formulating a plan. He could tell Jane was in the same condition. Once again, Charlie's presence was a tremendous relief to him. Charlie's calm pragmatism was exactly what they needed right now.

"What made you come here, Charlie? With all the excitement, I don't think you mentioned why you're here," asked Jane, breaking the silence.

"You failed to communicate during our designated time. I figured either you ran into a problem or the range was too far. In either case, since you weren't too far from Scott's house, I decided to check on you."

"We tried to call you for about an hour right after

midnight," said Jane. "How are Mike and Jenny? She obviously held up for the walk?"

"Barely. Scott and his wife desperately need supplies, so I'm not altogether too optimistic about the trip to HQ. They're looking definitively worse for the wear. I hoped to bring some more food back to them, but it doesn't look like anything has been left untouched around here."

"Everything has been ransacked by those animals," said Sam. "Thank you for coming. We were relieved to see you this afternoon, to say the least. I don't know if we can pull this off with just the two of us," said Sam. "If they come back again while we're in the house, we'd be in trouble. We got lucky with the gunshot. Tank probably got pissed and shot one of his crew when the car broke down."

"Sounded like a rifle shot to me," said Charlie.

Jane glanced at Sam with a knowing look, both of them blurting the same name at the same time.

"Mark."

"Mark?" said Charlie.

"He's a former Force Recon Marine turned attic dweller. He has a clean line of sight down the street. Sounds like he did us a big favor," said Sam.

"If we could get Mark in on this, we could even the odds with the element of surprise. Three against five isn't undoable, but it isn't great either," said Charlie, stretching out on the couch. "Plus, we don't know who else might arrive later tonight."

"We should signal him. God knows we could use his help. He's probably one of the most capable people we'll ever run into. It can't hurt to ask," said Sam.

"Yeah, you're right. But why would he want to get involved? A lot of people seem to be keeping their heads down, too afraid to stand up to the New Order. For good reason," said Charlie.

"He already has gotten involved. He didn't have to flag us down as we entered the neighborhood, nor did he have to slow down Tank and the guys while we were in the house," said Sam.

"I'll go up and shut the signal shade in the spare bedroom," said Jane, getting up.

Jane moved through the house quicker than she had before. Experience with the contours of the house allowed Jane to move quickly through its dark hallways. Crossing the front of the Cramers' house, Jane could see her home through a part in the curtain. Inside, a few dim lights cast an eerie glow to the once cheerful home. Silently, she prayed for help and for Lea. They would need all the help they could get.

Hearing a loud noise entering the neighborhood, Jane returned to the front window. A car turned down the street and headed toward their home. Three large New Order men got out of the car and joined their brethren inside. Eight against three, maybe four if Mark would help. A sick feeling crept over her. They needed Mark's help more than ever.

— 46 —

Mark had long since moved away from his post at the window. After he determined that the unknown operator was a friendly, he assumed Jane and Sam would wait for nightfall before returning to the Cramers' house. What he did not know was if they'd found their daughter. Lea had not been with them when they ran from the house following his warning shot. He could only assume Lea was not found. At this point, he figured that Jane and Sam had left the neighborhood. Why would they stay around? They'd indicated they knew of a place containing supplies. They'd probably waited until dark and started moving.

He went back to his usual duties, the excitement of the day passing. He took the waste bucket to the woods, checked the progress of the deer draining in the garage and then settled in for an early night.

Sleep eluded him as he considered how close he had come to shooting Jane and Sam's friend. The man was seconds from having his head blown off. Luckily, the man motioned to Jane and Sam in an obviously friendly manner, pulling them into the safety of his hiding spot. Before the grid went out, he would never have considered shooting a man in cold blood unless given orders in a lawful wartime situation. The world had changed, taking him with it.

Getting up from the makeshift bed, Mark sat quietly by the window. He'd grown fond of his perch. The bright full moon illuminated the clear sky, casting a bluish silvery glow over the houses. He loved the night. Looking out the window, over the quiet world, he could almost imagine things were back to normal.

Returning his gaze to the Cramers' house, Mark noticed a slight change in the façade. Looking through his spotting scope, Mark inspected the signal window. Someone had lowered the shade, indicating a need for help. Finally. He was tired of safely sitting in his attic, waiting for others to restore order.

Lifting the blanket off his arsenal, Mark stood looking at the weapons at his disposal, considering his options. Deciding for a full load out, Mark donned a tactical plate carrier loaded with rifle magazines and a ballistic helmet with attached night-vision goggles. He attached the AR-15 to a sling point on his vest and let it hang across his chest. For the first time since the lights went out, Mark felt a sense of direction, excitement and hope.

~ ~ ~

Sam heard Jane's footsteps as she returned to the basement. He was always amazed at her ability to walk in the dark. She rarely turned on the lights to walk through their own home.

"Everything quiet up there?" asked Charlie.

"Not really. I pulled the signal shade down no problem, but while I was up there, a car came into the neighborhood. Three more New Order men are in the house now."

"Shit. That makes eight. There's no way we can get in there with all of them inside," said Sam.

"I say we wait until tomorrow. Maybe they'll leave again. Then the two of you can go inside and cut Lea free while I watch over you, like we did today. In fact, I could move upstairs for a better view. I have my radio, so we can stay in contact," said Charlie.

"Assuming they leave again," said Sam.

"You're also assuming they won't kill Lea or harm her further tonight. We can't take that chance. We need to get her out of there as quickly as possible. Her life depends on it," said Jane. "You should have seen the conditions they're keeping her in. She's little more than a piece of trash at this point. A few shots of hard booze away from a death sentence—or worse."

"Sam, do you think with your hunting knife or my knife you can cut her free, or should we try to get more tools for you to use, just in case?"

"I can do it. It'll take a little time, mostly so I don't slice through her wrists, but I should be able to do it with my good knife. I didn't even think to bring it," said Sam.

"No one could have predicted that we would be in this situation. Don't be so hard on yourself," said Jane, wrapping her arms around him.

"I know, but I can't help thinking that if I'd brought both knives with me, we could have grabbed her and we would be out of here."

"It probably wouldn't have made a difference. We only had a few minutes with her before we had to bolt out of there. If you had tried to cut her loose, you might have done more harm than good. Who knows, you could have inadvertently hurt her," said Jane. "Or got through most of the rope, but not enough to get her free. Tank might have noticed."

"I know you're right, but still, it bothers me."

"How will your friend Mark get in? Did you leave a door open, Jane?" asked Charlie.

"No, I didn't think of it. Seeing the extra guys roll up to our house sort of threw me. Hold on, I'll be right back," said Jane, heading toward the steps.

— 47 —

Jane opened the rear sliding door, peering beyond the deck and into the yard, hopeful Mark would see the signal and come to them.

"Jane," someone whispered from a distance.

A slight rustling near the pines announced Mark's arrival.

"Boy, you are a sight for sore eyes. They have our daughter tied up in the basement of our home. We're trying to figure out how to get her out of there without getting us all killed. We could really use your help," said Jane.

"Definitely. I saw the signal and came as quickly as possible. I'm tired of sitting on the sidelines. I want to help in whatever way I can," said Mark.

"I can't tell you how much we appreciate this. Come on in, we're all in the basement."

In the basement, the four sat huddled around a flashlight, formulating a rescue mission.

"Jane, you definitely saw three men walk into the house earlier this evening?" asked Charlie.

"Yeah, it was right after I put down the shade to signal

Mark. On my way back to the basement, I passed the front window just as they came into the neighborhood."

"I'm surprised I missed that. I must've fallen asleep for a minute," said Mark.

"Okay, so here's the situation as we know it. We have eight or possibly more unfriendlies, potentially on multiple levels of the house, and a hostage in the basement. Correct?" asked Charlie.

"Yes. And we're sure there were only five men originally in the house. Jane and I sat watching them for nearly twenty-four hours before we went in yesterday. While in the house, we searched it from top to bottom. No one else is in there," added Sam.

"Well, that's good news. At least we have a firm headcount. That should make things a little easier," said Mark.

"Eight on four doesn't sound easy," said Sam.

"I think we need to draw all of them out into the yard and pick them off one at a time," said Jane. "Or a few at a time."

"Bingo," announced Mark.

"We just need to be sure none of them go back inside. We also need to be sure we don't hit the house. I wouldn't want Lea getting killed by a stray bullet from one of our guns," said Charlie. "She's in the basement, but bullets have a strange way of travelling and they could move her without our knowledge."

"How do we get them all out of the house at the same time?" asked Sam.

"That's the tricky part. We'll need two levels of distraction. The first will draw out some of the men. I assume they won't all pile out at once. Then a second to ensure the rest move outside and into the kill zone we've created. With the suppressed weapons, the second group won't have a good sense of what happened," said Mark.

"How do we get them out?" said Jane.

"I have a stash of fireworks at my house. We could light 'em up in the house next door to our current location, requiring the New Order guys to cross the street to check it out—directly in front of our guns," offered Mark.

"I like it. As they cross, we pick them off with suppressed fire. They won't know what hit them. With any luck, the remaining men inside won't see what happened to the first wave of men," said Charlie.

"While you two are doing that, if all the men haven't exited our house, I could shoot up the cars. I would think that might get the attention of anyone remaining in the house," said Jane.

"Don't you want to take one of those? It would be nice to drive to the storage locker instead of walk. Besides, Lea might not be able to walk very easily. You saw her condition. She's been shackled to that pole for so long, her legs might be too weak to make it. I managed to find a muscle relaxant in the aspirin bottle and gave that to her. It should help ease some of her pain, but still, I'm worried about her ability to move quickly," said Sam.

"All those times you would get on me for mixing pills into the aspirin bottle and it finally came in handy. I feel vindicated," said Jane, with a broad smile.

"Why would you do that?" asked Mark.

"So I could just pack one bottle when we travel. The New Order guys probably never would have thought to inspect each aspirin."

"No one would, really. The whole thing is a bad idea," said Sam, shaking his head.

Mark shook his head, concurring with Sam's statement.

"I don't think driving out of here is a good idea, regardless of Lea's condition. The only people in town who drive are the New Order men. Everything is so quiet now without the constant buzzing of cars and machines. You won't get out of the greater neighborhood before they either hear or see you on the road. Then you're screwed," said Mark. "And what's all this about a storage locker?"

"Jane and I keep a backup of our readiness supplies in a storage locker at Store-Right on Michigan. We plan to head there to resupply and possibly stay for a while until we figure out our next move."

"That's clever. Keeping everything at the house makes sense in most disaster scenarios, but spreading it out gives you extra flexibility…you know, in case a nearby prison disgorges several hundred felony convicts into your community. Thanks mostly to these New Order thugs, most people's supplies are totally gone. You two might be the only people with any sort of gear at your disposal," said Mark.

"You're welcome to come with us. We have more than enough for all five of us," said Jane.

"We probably have enough for twenty," said Sam. "And we can't possibly cart a fraction of it out of there, so you're welcome to take what you want while you decide on your next move."

"I plan to go with them, at least for a little while," said Charlie.

Jane thought it was interesting that Charlie failed to mention the HQ or safe houses to Mark. She knew Charlie would be returning to Scott's as soon as Lea was extracted. She wondered why he would leave Mark out of the loop. Probably a trust issue, which gave her an uneasy feeling. They had to be a little more careful with whom they entrusted their secrets.

"Alright. Sounds like a plan," said Mark. "I'll take you up on the resupply offer and decide what to do from there."

"Let's get back to the plan for a minute. Is everyone clear about their role?" Charlie pointed at the crude map of the street flattened on the coffee table. "Mark, you're setting off firecrackers in this house."

"That's the Spencers' house," said Jane.

"I'll be at the front door of the Cramers' house, with the door open a crack," said Charlie, tapping his finger.

"After the firecrackers go off, I'll move to this position," said Mark, indicating a point on the map.

Mark would cleverly position himself so that he could shoot any of the men who made it past Charlie, without hitting Charlie in the crossfire. Sam joined the discussion, placing his index finger on the Archers' garage.

"Before any of this goes down, Jane and I will cross the street way out of sight and make our way here, where we can observe the side door to the house and the backyard in case anyone bolts out of the slider on the deck. If all eight of them aren't taken down in front of the house, we'll start shooting out tires or whatever we can hit on the cars."

"Once all of the men are out of the house and neutralized, Sam and I will go in and get Lea," said Jane.

"I'm having second thoughts about you going inside," said Mark.

"Me or Sam?" said Jane.

"Both of you, to be honest," said Mark.

"I've cleared houses before—in the dark," said Jane. "Sam has the least experience here."

"I understand that, but my guess is that Sam is handier with a knife," said Mark. "And we need to get Lea untied and back outside quickly. Unless we get extremely lucky and take all eight of them down with suppressed shots, their return fire will be heard throughout the town. In the past, any kind of noise drew other New Order men into the mix. It seems like they're just waiting around for trouble. Nothing says trouble like live fire. I wouldn't be surprised if several cars arrived before the gunfight ended. I recommend that Jane lights the fireworks and runs out the back door to a position here between the Spencers' and Cramers' houses, where you and Charlie can provide over-watch while Sam and I go in to get Lea," said Mark.

"Alright. You're right. That's a better plan," said Jane reluctantly.

She didn't like the idea of being separated from Sam or Lea. However, the house would be pitch dark. Mark's night vision and close-quarters battle training would tip the scale in their favor if things went awry with the original plan. They might also need to carry Lea out of the house, and Mark would be better suited for that task.

"I feel better about this. When the first wave of men start filtering out, I can be on the south side of Jane's house, here," said Mark, pointing on the map. "That enables me to help Charlie pick off the men that rush outside, and get to Sam for round two."

"Exactly," said Charlie.

"It's settled, then. I'll dash back to my place and grab the firecrackers. The rest of you should get your gear together and be ready to move out as soon as I get back," said Mark excitedly. "I suggest you pack up everything you want to take out of here, because we're probably looking at a grab-and-go situation when the shooting stops."

— 48 —

The group huddled together on the floor of the Spencers' living room. Mark delivered a duffel bag filled with assorted fireworks. It was the largest selection Charlie had ever seen. Although Charlie was slow to warm up to anyone new, especially in this changed world, he couldn't help but admire Mark. However, liking and trusting were two different things. He needed to be sure about Mark before he felt comfortable sharing the location of the safe houses and HQ. Charlie was grateful that Jane went along with his small lie about where he would go after the extraction. He had no intention of staying at the storage locker longer than required to stuff his backpack with the supplies that he intended to give to Scott and his family.

"We need to join the wicks to make them as long as possible," said Mark.

"Why? It seems like we're risking that the wicks may not stay lit," said Sam.

"I don't think one round of firecrackers is enough. We need to set off the first round. Give them time to get up and then start setting off the second and third rounds. That way they know exactly where to go. If we just set off the first round, by the time they look outside, they might not catch where the noise came from. That would be a disaster," said Mark.

"We could have all of the New Order men walking around in different directions. We need to avoid that," said Charlie.

"I'm glad you guys are helping us. This is a great plan. I'm starting to feel confident about getting Lea back," said Jane.

"Don't thank us yet. A lot can go wrong in a short stretch of time," said Mark.

Tying the last wick, Charlie said, "That should do it."

"Come on, Jane, let's get these set up," said Mark, grabbing the first string.

"The ones with the longest wicks will go into the dining room; then we'll put the medium-length wicks into the living room and the shortest ones right here—in the front window. You're going to set off all three simultaneously, starting with the longest wick," said Mark.

"Got it. If I go quickly enough, the length of the wicks should space out the noise, creating a long chain of blasts," said Jane.

"That's the idea. We're hoping to grab their attention and draw them in."

"I've never really blown off firecrackers before. Never been into them. What do you think will happen to the inside of the house?" asked Jane.

"Let's put it this way, the Spencers could very well be out of a house. The fountains will likely catch the place on fire," said Mark.

"Can't we just stick to the firecracker things?" said Jane. "I hate doing that to them."

"The fountains will really attract their attention. They might even guess that a fire broke out in the basement and ignited the family's Fourth of July stash. I wouldn't be surprised if they dragged out some chairs and watched the show."

"Wouldn't that be nice," said Sam. "We could gun them down all in one place."

"I'm not counting on it," said Charlie. "Jane, if you're ready, we need to get in position." Charlie glanced at Mark and Sam.

"I'm set. What could go wrong?" said Jane, with a sarcastic tone.

Walking to Jane, Sam embraced her tightly. "I love you, you know."

"I know, and love you more. Now go rescue our baby," said Jane, pulling away from his embrace.

"Jane, you'll be on your own without a radio. Mark and I will be communicating throughout, adjusting the plan if needed. Under no circumstance are you to leave your covered position until one of us signals or yells that it's clear. No matter what happens, we meet at the end of the street, near the woods," said Charlie.

"Got it," said Jane.

"I know those woods really well. With the moonlight's help, we should have no problem cutting through to get to Michigan Road," said Mark.

"Alright—let's do this," said Jane.

Charlie and Mark walked out first. Sam took one more look over his shoulder at Jane and then slowly closed the door behind him.

— 49 —

From her perch near the window, Jane watched the shadowy figures of Mark and Sam sprint across the street to get into their positions. A few minutes after they vanished into the darkness, Mark appeared at the back corner of the Archers' house and crawled down the southern face of the house to a spot several feet back from the front corner. Once Mark and Sam were in position, Charlie would signal Mark that he was ready. Then, when everyone was situated, Mark would flash a small light, giving Jane the "thumbs-up" to start lighting the wicks.

Jane breathed rapidly, waiting for Mark's signal. She refused to allow herself to ponder the fact that they were lining up to kill these men in a cold-blooded ambush. The men were vicious killers who had destroyed the lives of her friends, neighbors and fellow police officers. Even after the police took back the town and things returned to normal, it would take a very long time to heal the collective wounds inflicted by these jackbooted murderers. Tonight was just the first of many necessary steps they would all take to smash down this supposed New Order.

Staring intently at Mark's position, Jane thought she had somehow missed the signal. It seemed like an eternity since he'd settled into a prone firing position. Finally, a faint light flashed on and off.

It's time.

Jane's hands trembled as she touched the longest wick and clicked the lighter. The wick took immediately in a golden glow of fire. The flame effortlessly moved down the extended wick with such speed that Jane began to doubt their plan. She raced to the next bundle, lighting the flame before she arrived. She needed to get all three lit before bolting out of the house.

The second wick ignited immediately, racing toward the collection of fireworks. *Shit!* Jane barreled through the house to the front corner room, locating the fireworks in the center of the coffee table. She clicked the lighter. Once, twice, three times. Nothing. *No! No! Click. Click. Damn it!* Finally a flame. Jane held the wick to the flame and tried to steady herself. Her hands trembled violently, making it hard to align the flame with the waiting fuse.

She glanced up, staring through the front window of the Spencers' house. A New Order man stood on her front stoop across the street, lighting a cigarette. If the man looked up, he would see her in the window. Jane focused her concentration on steadying her hands and lighting the wick.

The flame licked the edges of the wick, gently touching it but not igniting the short wick. Each time Jane glanced up to the smoking man, she lost the connection to the wick and had to reignite the lighter. *Click. Click.* She had nearly resigned herself to the fact that the other fireworks would go off while she was in the house.

Her hand suddenly steadied. *Click.* Flame. The gunpowder-laced wick sparked, the short length blazing toward the fireworks. Jane looked up again, her face illuminated by the glowing flame, just as the man looked up in her direction. A moment of confusion seemed to cross the man's face.

Jane peeled herself from the front window and sprinted through the back door of the house. The ear-piercing sound of explosions and shrieking fireworks followed her out, setting their plan in motion. She quickly reached the back corner of the Spencers' house. Waiting for the first round of shooting to start, Jane disengaged the safety on her AR-15 and aimed in the direction of the street.

~ ~ ~

Roscoe stood on the front stoop of the house, smoking a cigarette. He intended to enjoy every last smoke he could get his hands on. Supplies were getting thinner by the day. They'd partied so hard the first week, now they had to ration the supplies, including cigarettes. Of course, Tank always ate and smoked his fill. *Asshole.* Roscoe hated Tank. He had no idea why that loser was in charge. He took a drag on his cigarette, knowing Tank's time was measured. One bullet and Roscoe was the new chief. He just had to time it right.

Until then, he'd keep a low profile. Life could be worse. He could be a civilian. A regular Joe that used to own one of these houses. Man, had they taught these assholes a lesson. The New Order owned this town. No cops was the best part. He would never have to go back to another shithole PrisCorp prison. He had no idea what had knocked out the electricity, and he didn't care. It had been the best thing ever.

Something drew his gaze to the house across the street. The house was empty, they'd made sure of that, but every once in a while they found a squatter. He probably imagined what he saw. Only an idiot would pick a house right across the street from them to squat in. His eyes caught movement again. Focusing on the front corner window, he saw a woman's face.

No shit? Some people are just too dumb to live.

The room burst into light as loud explosions shattered the silent night. The door behind him flew open. He stood watching, mesmerized by the colorful light show inside.

"What the fuck is going on out there?" yelled Tank from inside the house.

"Fireworks in the house across the street! Thought I saw someone over there!"

"Get over there and check it out! All of you!" screamed Tank.

Roscoe and four other New Order men stood in the center of the lawn, watching the fireworks show, unsure what to make of it.

"This ain't the Fourth of July, you fucking assholes! Lock this shit down!" said Tank, appearing in the doorway.

Moving cautiously, the men crossed the yard, heading toward the street.

— 50 —

Mark lay flat on his stomach in the Archers' side yard, his rifle trained forward. When the fireworks started, he waited patiently, resisting every urge to crawl forward and start shooting. He had to trust Charlie's judgment. If too many men ran out at once, Charlie would let them drift far enough across the front yard to enter Mark's field of fire. That way, they could coordinate a simultaneous crossfire. He stared over the red dot sight, willing the men to appear. With the fireworks burning brightly in the Spencers' house, the New Order soldiers would be perfectly silhouetted.

For all he knew, Charlie had started firing already. The firecrackers created an incredible racket. Just as he was about to slither forward, a partially illuminated figure moved into his kill zone. The size of the group grew as they approached the Spencers' house. Five men. They could do this.

As previously agreed, Mark centered his red dot sight on the last man's lower cranial area and fired. The bullet hit the man squarely in the neck, dropping him instantly. The man's crumpled body lay motionless in the yard, unnoticed by the four men creeping toward the fireworks display.

Lining up the next man in his sights, Mark fired again, striking the man in the head. Strangely, he didn't go down like the first man. He stumbled forward, still clutching his rifle. Before Mark could take another shot, the street exploded in gunfire—the crippled man's rifle emptying its magazine into the pavement.

All bets were off as pandemonium descended on the kill zone. Charlie hit one of the men in the shoulder, causing him to spin around and fire into the man behind him. Mark assumed the lead man either saw Charlie or saw Charlie's fire, because he moved with a purpose toward the Cramers' front door, shooting as he went. The man's bullets hit the side of the front of the house, splintering wood and shattering windows on both sides of the door.

Mark compensated for the man's movement, placing the red dot right in front of the man. He squeezed the trigger repeatedly until the man tumbled to the ground. The gunfire continued for a few more seconds, Charlie's suppressed rifle snapping bullet after bullet into the remaining men.

When the shooting stopped, silence blanketed the macabre moonlit spectacle. Glancing around the carnage in the yard, Mark quickly counted—four confirmed kills. The fifth man was still alive, dragging himself across the yard, desperately trying to make it back into the perceived safety of the house. He moaned loudly, calling out for his New Order buddies.

He started to track the man with his rifle sight, but the target's profile was too low to the ground to score a lethal hit. Charlie would have to finish this. Mark needed to link up with Sam immediately.

~ ~ ~

Jane sat across the street from her house, hidden behind a brick chimney. She saw Mark take off toward the back of the house, heading to meet Sam. Together, they would find Lea. When the last of the fireworks detonated, the street went quiet except for the awful sound of a man in agony. She leaned a few inches to her right, finding the source of the misery. A man was clawing and scrambling his way to the front door of the Archers' house, coughing and choking.

"Sorry," she whispered, centering the man's creeping form in the red circle of her rifle sight. "No survivors tonight."

The Archers' front door flew open, Tank's hulking silhouette appearing deep in the shadowy recesses of the doorframe. Tank fired his rifle from the hip on full automatic, pounding away at the front of the Cramers' house for a few seconds before shifting his fire to Jane. She dropped to the ground and pressed against the house as bullets tore through the brick, spraying her with stone and powder.

The gun went silent, daring her to take a peek. When she poked her head around the corner, she saw Tank reloading the rifle. One shot and she could end this. Before she could move, he charged the rifle and fired a long burst in Charlie's direction. Tank had that killing machine under good control, which was more than Jane could say for her own shaky hands. She willed her rifle up into her shoulder, hoping to squeeze off a shot before he turned the rifle on her.

Instead of sending the remains of his magazine in her direction, he stopped. The dying man crawling up the stoop lifted a shaking hand toward Tank and begged him for help. Tank emptied his rifle into the man at point-blank range, showering the sidewalk in blood.

"You're next, motherfuckers!" shouted Tank.

He slammed the door shut before she could press the trigger.

~ ~ ~

Sam watched as the scene unfolded in the front yard. His position allowed him to safely watch the action, out of the line of fire, but he could not effectively shoot into the men without sending bullets toward the Cramers' house. A quick body count indicated that three men remained active threats. He didn't see who killed the last man crawling across the yard, but the fusillade had come from inside the house. Whoever was left in their home was on a murderous rampage. Mark hadn't arrived, but he needed to initiate the second part of the plan immediately. Lea's life most certainly depended on it.

Nestling into the AR-15, Sam flipped the safety to fire, keeping his eyes on the side door to the house. Without Mark to cover the door, he'd have to split his attention. Now he wished he had listened to Jane and taken one of those tactical rifle classes. Sam could fire accurately, but his experience did not extend beyond shooting paper targets at the range. Hopefully, that was all he'd need. He aimed at one of the cars visible from the corner of the garage, pressing the trigger.

~ ~ ~

Tank angrily paced the living room. Five of his men were dead, leaving him with just the two blank-faced idiots without an idea between them. If he intended to get out of here, he needed to act fast. His first instinct was to make a stand and wait for reinforcements, but whoever had taken down his crew had used suppressed weapons. This was the work of professionals. They'd hit the house hard and fast, leaving him dead. He needed to break out of here before they assembled for some kind of SWAT-like break-in.

Sharp cracking sounds exploded outside the house, causing him to crouch. He raised his rifle, listening intently, immediately recognizing the hiss of tires and the hollow punching of bullets through thin metal. *They're taking out the cars!* He started to move toward the side door of the house, but stopped. *Why aren't they shooting into the house? Why didn't they light him up when he opened the door? They didn't want to shoot into the house. That's why!*

"It's that dumb bitch, Lea!" Tank shouted excitedly.

"What is? What do you mean?" asked the man named Chill.

"They want Lea! I bet her cop momma is out there right now, directing the show. Well, if she wants her, she can have her!" shouted Tank, his heavy feet pounding toward the basement stairs.

Tank rushed into the pitch-black darkness of the basement, wielding a large hunting knife. He shone a flashlight at Lea's grimy face, wondering why he hadn't gutted her earlier.

"I knew there was a reason I didn't kill you! You're finally worth something to me, you dumb bitch!" shrieked Tank.

Yanking her up to her feet by her hair, Tank began to slice through the ropes.

"You're cutting me!" screamed Lea in pain.

"Shut the fuck up!"

The knife effortlessly sliced through the ropes and her skin, freeing Lea. Tank dragged her upstairs and through the house by her hair, joining his men in the kitchen.

"The two of you follow me to the pickup. They don't want to shoot this one," said Tank, thrusting Lea in front of him.

Blood dripped freely from her arms, pooling on the hardwood floor in front of the stunned men.

"No fucking way I'm walking out of here. Didn't you see what they did to Roscoe and the others? We don't even know how many there are! I'm staying. It's only a matter of time before the others get here!" said Chill, crossing his arms over his chest.

"Whatever works best for you," said Tank.

In one swift movement, Tank dropped the hunting knife in his hand and pulled a pistol from the small of his back. He took a single step forward and shot Chill through the sternum. The dumbfounded gang member stumbled backward into the refrigerator, his limp body sliding down to a seated position on the floor. Lea screamed uncontrollably until Tank aimed the gun at her.

"Shut the fuck up," he stated. "Or you're next."

She nodded meekly, tears running down her dirty cheeks.

"How about you?" asked Tank, shifting the gun to the remaining man.

"I guess I'm driving," said Salem, grabbing the keys from the dirty table.

— 51 —

Sam fired methodically, disabling each vehicle within view. He leaned beyond the corner a little further and spotted the Trans Am. He'd rather shoot Tank, but this would do for now. Just as the first bullets started pinging off the side of the vehicle, the side door to the house burst open. Lea appeared in the doorway, one of Tank's muscular, tattooed arms wrapped tightly across her chest. He half lifted, half dragged her onto the driveway.

Sam aimed his rifle in their direction, with zero intention of attempting a shot.

"Shoot me or shoot her! Your choice, asshole!" shouted Tank.

Shit! This wasn't part of the plan.

A second man walked closely behind Tank, trying his best to stay hidden. Lea's bare feet dragged on the ground, making it obvious that she was not walking on her own. Blood dripped from her thin arms.

That asshole cut her ropes and shredded her arms in the process!

Anger consumed Sam, emboldening him. He closed one eye and tried to center the rifle sight on Tank's face, but Lea's head bobbed unpredictably in and out of the way. There was no way he could do this.

Movement from the Archers' backyard caught Sam's attention. He could barely make out Mark's dark form as he rounded the corner of the house. A single flash and snapping sound from Mark's rifle dropped the man closely following Tank and Lea. Tank barely noticed. He just kept pushing Lea toward the truck. Sam felt powerless. Mark obviously didn't feel comfortable with the shot either. Mark's rifle, like his own, helplessly followed Tank and Lea as they drew closer to an undamaged pickup truck.

"No! I will not go with you!" screamed Lea.

She worked her feet and legs up the side of the truck, pushing herself back into Tank and nearly tipping him over. True to his name, Tank didn't topple. He quickly regained his balance and pummeled the side of her head with his free hand until her legs dangled uselessly under her. Before Sam knew it, Tank had opened the driver's side door and shoved her inside—piling in with her.

The engine roared to life, jarring Sam and Mark into action. At nearly the same moment, Sam and Mark fired single shots at the tires, hoping to end the truck's journey before it left the driveway. Nothing seemed to work. The truck screeched onto the street and gained speed on its flattened tires.

Charlie and Jane ran toward the street in a mad effort to stop the pickup truck. Charlie passed Jane, sprinting with a pistol in his hand. He got within a few feet of the driver's side window, extending the pistol, before the truck burst forward, opening the distance. They all met in the middle of the street, lungs heaving from the failed effort. Just like that, Sam realized their daughter was gone.

~ ~ ~

Lea sat in the front seat of the pickup truck, desperately trying to figure out a way to get away from Tank. Her mom had taught her never to allow herself to be taken to a secondary location by an assailant. A kidnap victim's chance of survival dropped significantly after being taken from the scene of the abduction. If she was going to survive the night, she needed to do something now, before they left the neighborhood.

She started to sob while slowly and carefully inching her way across the seat toward the passenger's side door. *Slowly, slowly, just a little more.* Moving her hand an inch at a time, Lea finally managed to grasp the handle of the door.

"Tank?" she said.

"What?" he grunted.

"Go fuck yourself," she said, opening the door and dropping out of the pickup truck in one smooth motion.

She hit the pavement with an unexpected violence, rolling and skidding along the rough surface until coming to a pained stop. The pickup truck came to a screeching halt thirty yards down the road. Glancing back toward her neighborhood, she prayed he'd keep on driving. No such luck. The white reverse lights illuminated the pavement.

Scrambling to her feet, Lea hobbled in the direction of her neighborhood, moving faster than she thought possible after hitting the road so hard. The pickup truck backed up, picking up speed. Moments before the truck hit her, she darted left, out of the road. The pickup truck continued past, into a maelstrom of bullets.

She crawled as fast as she could away from the street as four figures ran down the middle of the road, rapidly firing as they closed the gap to the truck. Bullets thunked into Tank's pickup, shattering the rear window and blasting the passenger-side mirror into pieces. The onslaught lasted a few more seconds before the truck lurched forward, racing out of the neighborhood.

"Mom!" shouted Lea. "Dad!"

In the distance, Lea could hear cars headed in their direction. New Order reinforcements were on the way.

"We have to move, keep running toward our house!" shouted her mother.

Two heavily armed men swooped in to provide protective cover as Lea, Jane and Sam barreled toward them.

"We need to get out of here fast! They're coming!" shouted one of the men.

"Can you keep running?" asked her mom.

"Are you badly injured?" said her dad.

He quickly bear-hugged her and kissed her forehead before taking up a position in the perimeter formed by the two military-looking men. She thought she recognized one of them from the department, but couldn't be sure.

"Yes! I'm fine. We need to go!" screamed Lea.

She couldn't believe she was alive. It hurt to run, but she knew it was the only way they would survive. She wanted nothing more than to hold her mom and dad, but that could wait.

The five of them ran as quickly as possible through the neighborhood, grabbing backpacks and spare weapons from a pile behind the Cramers' house before heading into the woods. The shadows from the trees and underbrush concealed them from the mayhem unfolding on the street.

"Where are we going?" asked Lea.

"To the storage unit on Michigan," said Sam.

"We need to regroup, get supplies and then head out of town," said Jane.

"No! We need to get as far away from here as possible. They'll kill all of us. It isn't safe here!" hissed Lea.

Her dad placed his warm hand on her shoulder, looking her straight in the eyes. "We'll be okay. We're together now, and that's all that matters. Remember the storage unit? We have everything we need there, and we will be safe. Plus, we have two guardian angels to keep a close watch over us."

Sam always calmed Lea.

"Who are they?" said Lea.

"You might remember Charlie from one of the police department picnics. He's a good friend of your mother's. The guy walking point is Mark Jordan, one of our neighbors. Just so happens he's a Force Recon Marine."

"What's that?" asked Lea.

"A badass. Your dad used to patch them up when they exceeded their badass quotient," said Jane.

"I heard that," said a voice out of sight in front of them.

"Looks like all of you are badasses," said Lea.

"Are you kidding me? You jumped out of a moving vehicle. I'd say you're in the right club," said her mother.

"Damn right," said Lea.

— 52 —

Sam walked a few feet behind Lea. He'd checked her wounds during their last stop. The blood from the cuts had slowed to a trickle thanks to the gauze he had taped around her wrists. Beyond that, she didn't show any permanent signs of damage. He'd feared a concussion, but she'd somehow escaped the fall from Tank's pickup truck with nothing more than a few scratches and a lot of sore spots. She'd be bruised all over, but that appeared to be the extent of it. He greatly admired his daughter's resilience and bravery. Not many people would have thrown themselves out of a moving truck.

Moving quickly down Michigan Road, Sam knew they needed to stay concealed, but wished they could get there faster. He wanted to clean his daughter's wounds and get her fed. She'd been through a terrible ordeal. A few minutes later, Store-Right's large sign came into sight. Unlit, it stood as a dark contrast to the night sky. Relief washed over Sam. He'd half expected the place to be burned to the ground. For the first time since they'd come out of the mountains, he started to believe they would make it.

"Jane, is this the place?" asked Mark over his shoulder to Jane.

"That's it. We're on the south side, unit 52L," said Jane.

"It's around the back side of the property. Once we get into the fenced area, we should be fine. No one will be able to see us from the street," said Sam.

"Alright, let's stop here. We need to conduct a little surveillance before we go in. Just to be sure no one sees us from the outside—or inside," said Charlie.

The group huddled between two parked cars in the neighboring strip mall. The deserted mall, with its smashed-out windows and looted shadowy interiors, sat as a stark reminder of a past life, creepy and desolate. Sam wanted to get out of there as quickly as possible.

"How long do you want to wait before we go in?" asked Sam.

"Not sure yet. It's best to hang back—listen and look," said Mark.

"Hopefully, not more than ten to fifteen minutes," said Sam.

"How can we get in? The entire facility is surrounded by a high chain-link fence topped with barbed wire," said Jane.

"I brought steel cutters. They can get through anything. I recommend we go to that spot, there." Mark pointed. "Make a small cut and slip through. Nobody will notice it during the day."

"Good call. It's the perfect spot. Close enough to the forest if we need to leave in a hurry," said Charlie.

"Let's be ready to move in ten," said Mark. "That should give us enough time."

"You still okay, sweetie?" asked Jane, turning to Lea.

"I'm good, just super thirsty," said Lea. "And hungry."

"We have plenty of food in the locker," said Jane.

After waiting longer than Sam thought possible, the group moved in a tight formation toward the spot picked by Mark. Mark quickly pulled out his steel cutters and cut a three-foot slit in the fence.

"I'll cut just a little more; then we'll need to bend it back. I want to keep it intact so we can bend it back in place once inside. That way, from the road, no one will know we breached the fence," said Mark as he snipped a few more links. Each of them passed through the narrow opening, mindful of the fence's jagged edges.

"Come on, this way, it's just around back," Sam said excitedly.

Finally arriving at unit 52L, Lea sat down heavily on the hard pavement, waiting for Sam to open the door.

— 53 —

Sam turned the padlock's dial quickly, opening the lock within seconds. Instead of immediately lifting the heavy metal sliding door, Sam moved his hands along the seam between the door and the metal frame of the building.

"What are you doing?" asked Charlie.

"Do you need help lifting the door?" asked Mark.

"Nope. I'm removing the bolts I placed to keep the door from opening freely. I drilled a hole in each side. The bolts slide into the track on the inside, freezing the door in place. I figured that if this day came, others might try to break in and look for stuff. Cutting a padlock is one thing, but trying to fix a jammed door might make this locker not worth the trouble," said Sam.

He pulled a flat-headed, five-inch-long bolt from each side of the door before heaving the door open. The door rolled open, revealing a floor-to-ceiling wall of used furniture, boxes, cabinets, old lamps and other assorted junk. To the casual observer, Sam wanted the locker to look like it was filled to the brim with old, used household goods. Useless stuff. Judging by the reactions he got from the group, he knew he'd accomplished that mission.

"Geez, Dad. What is all this crap?" asked Lea.

"Not to sound ungrateful, Sam," started Charlie, "but I don't think we can fit inside."

"Ye of little faith," said Sam. "Step inside, quickly. I'll pull the door down behind us."

The group stepped into the narrow space, against the seemingly impenetrable wall of discarded junk. As soon as everyone was just inside the locker, Sam quickly lowered the door, plunging them into darkness.

As though orchestrated, Sam, Jane, Charlie and Mark illuminated the dark space with their flashlights. Sam pulled out a small box hiding in the corner of the unit, near the door. The box contained a set of two blocks and clamps. Using a small step stool, Sam jammed the blocks into the top of the door's tracks and then clamped them in place so the door was jammed shut from the inside.

"There, that's better. Now let me move some of this out of the way so we can get into the real locker area," said Sam.

Sam pushed against a shoulder-height metal filing cabinet on the left side of the wall of junk, moving it a few feet toward the back of the unit. The metal cabinet moved easily enough, as though it was empty. He crouched low and disappeared into the space left by the cabinet, easily shifting it to the right and clearing a pathway deeper into the unit.

"This is so cool!" said Lea.

"Ingenious, really," said Mark. "Even if someone managed to break in, they'd be unlikely to figure this out."

"Yeah, I'm pretty happy with how it came out. I wanted it to be a sort of hideaway in case we needed to stay somewhere temporarily," said Sam, with obvious pride.

"Why didn't I know about all of this?" asked Lea.

"We told you, but I think this is the sort of thing that went in one ear and out the other," said Jane. "Like a lot of our parenting advice."

"Yeah, or barely in one ear," added Sam with a chuckle.

"Wow. I really had no idea what you were doing out here with this locker. I knew you had stuff here, but not much else," said Lea.

Sam hoped she'd never mentioned the storage locker to Tank. He didn't want to bring it up right now, but eventually he'd have to ask. Tank would likely turn over the entire town looking for her. If there was any chance she had mentioned it to him, their time here would be limited.

"Is this the same unit we've always had? It seems bigger somehow," said Jane.

"I upgraded to the biggest unit they have. Once I started moving stuff in here, it seemed to shrink. This one has the most floor space of any of the options offered by the facility. I even thought about claiming the one next to it for overflow," said Sam. "Just waiting for it to become available."

The unit was stuffed floor to ceiling with neatly labeled, clear waterproof supply bins. Boxes containing clothing, medical supplies, shoes, and foul-weather gear sat piled high against one of the walls. Large plastic jerry cans of water lined the opposite side wall. The entire back wall of the unit was stocked floor to ceiling with containers of dried foods and industrial-sized cans of beans, vegetables and fruit. The locker easily held a few years of food and enough water to hide out for a few weeks before venturing out to one of the nearby retention ponds.

Three mountain bikes fitted with side packs and tow trailers hung from the grated ceiling. Other supplies, like batteries, camping gear, cooking pots and a cooking stove sat neatly stacked on shelving units in the middle of the space. Sam pushed the filing cabinet back into place and slid a heavy dumbbell into place behind it.

Two long shower curtains hung from the grated ceiling in the back left corner of the storage unit, touching the floor and forming a square privacy area.

"What's behind the curtain?" said Mark.

"Compost toilet with stacks of organic material," said Sam. "Even supplied it with some old issues of *Popular Mechanics*."

"Nobody is spending enough time behind that curtain to read an article," said Jane, eliciting a round of laughter.

"Well, I'll be the first to say it. This place is amazing," announced Mark.

"Incredible," said Charlie. "What can we do to help?"

"We can start by setting up some cots. We could all use a little break."

Sam and Charlie started breaking out the camping cots, unfolding them next to the fake wall of junk at the front of the unit.

When they finished, he turned to Lea. "Lie down right there, Lea. I want to clean and re-dress your wounds."

"I'm fine, Dad. I'm not even bleeding anymore."

"Nice try. No way we're going to risk an infection. We don't have the luxury of taking you to the emergency room. Let me put new bandages and a nice thick coating of antibacterial gel on it," said Sam.

Sam retrieved a large medical supply bin, looking for the right combination of items to help his daughter.

"I'll put together a quick meal while you take care of Lea," said Jane, turning her attention to the wall of food. "Help yourself to some fresh water, or sort of fresh water. I'm not sure how long it has been in here."

"It's fresh. I have a rotation system that I loosely follow for the water, food and medical supplies," said Sam.

"How long have you been working on this place?" asked Charlie.

"I started stocking up at home several years ago, but then it occurred to me that putting all of our eggs in one basket might not be the best idea. I figured that if something bad enough happened that we truly needed to live off our supplies, we might need to do it quietly, away from home. That's when I decided to move the bulk of our stuff here and purchase the bikes and trailers for mobility," said Sam, finishing Lea's dressing. "If our house was still an option, we could transfer stuff back and forth, or just take off for a safer location."

"You were right about that. All this stuff would have been taken by the New Order if you had kept it at your house," said Mark.

"Who were those guys? Why are there so many of them?" asked Lea. "Some of the guys at the house were not part of Tank's original crew."

"They're escaped prisoners from the PrisCorp penitentiary about ten miles east of Evansville," said Charlie.

"Once the power failed, they just walked out, straight toward our towns. Porter was hit the worst. Things are very desperate over there," said Jane.

"I had no idea either until your parents told me. When things started getting crazy, I just retreated to my attic and kept a low profile. It has been hard to know who to trust," said Mark. "I wonder if anyone really knows what happened."

"I stayed put too, hoping for the best and waiting for you guys to come home. When Tank showed up, I knew that was a mistake," said Lea.

Lea's mention of Tank caused Sam to bristle. He saw that his wife had stiffened at the name, too. Their daughter had been through so much at his hands both before and after the lights went out.

"I'm so relieved we got you out of there," said Jane, sitting on the concrete floor next to Lea.

"Not more relieved than I am. Believe me," said Lea, turning to Mark. "You live in our neighborhood?"

"Yeah. One street over on Sequoya."

Jane set out a few battery-powered lanterns, creating a warm glow in the otherwise cold, industrial storage unit. She also handed out MREs to the hungry, tired group. Sam approved. Normally, they'd save the conveniently packaged MREs for travel, but they were far more satisfying than the freeze-dried stuff, and they didn't require boiled water. Each MRE came with a self-heating pack.

"You are both welcome to stay as long as you need. We have plenty of supplies, as you can see," said Sam.

"I'm with Sam. We really owe you guys. There is no way we would have been able to get Lea out of there without your help," added Jane.

"We have to stick together," said Charlie. "That's the only way we're going to survive this mess and put everything right again."

Sam could sense the gears turning in Jane's mind. Charlie was right. If everyone went their own way, groups like the New Order would come and go as they please, tearing what little remained of civil society apart. They all had to make a stand at some point—the sooner the better. He just wanted some time to let their daughter recover. A few weeks. Maybe several days. Somehow, he didn't think they had that much time before the situation spiraled beyond the point of no return.

~ ~ ~

After they finished eating, a quiet, food-induced haze descended on the group. Lea stretched out on one of the camp cots. Under the wool blanket Sam stretched over her, she quickly fell fast asleep. Jane moved closer to their daughter, sitting by the cot, gently rubbing Lea's head as she slept. When she was sure Lea was sound asleep, she joined her husband at a folding table at the back of the unit. Charlie and Mark were busy stuffing their backpacks with food. Jane had insisted that Charlie bring as much food as possible to the Marshes.

"What's the plan, guys?" said Jane. "Looks like you're getting ready to shove off."

"I need to get back to Scott Marsh's house. I left Mike and Jenny Sparr there. They'll be worried about me if I don't get back sooner rather than later," said Charlie.

"How soon?" asked Jane. "You could use a little more rest."

"Within the hour. I don't want Mike thinking he needs to put together a rescue team on my behalf. The sooner I get there, the better."

"How far away is Scott's house?" asked Mark.

"About a three-hour, fast-paced hike—if all goes well," said Charlie.

"You shouldn't go alone, not tonight, after everything that happened. The New Order could be out actively looking for us. It's too dangerous," said Jane.

"I agree, but tomorrow will be worse. At least I can use the night for cover. Once I get into the woods, I can head east. It's almost a straight shot," said Charlie.

"I'll go. That is, if you'll have me," offered Mark.

"Really? You don't have to. I got here and can get back, no problem," said Charlie.

"True. But I don't intend to sit on the sidelines anymore. I want to be a part of whatever is happening," said Mark. "If there's a war coming, count me in."

"I'd be glad to have you, Mark. Let's rest for an hour or so, then head out. It will be around midnight when we leave. As we get closer, I can use the radio to let them know we're coming."

"What happens at Scott's house?" asked Mark.

"Ideally, we grab Mike and Jenny and head out to the HQ at daybreak. We're assembling in Clark, just over the Grant line to the northeast," said Charlie.

"The HQ is in that area? If I recall correctly, there isn't much but forest and Lake Sparrow," said Mike.

"You're right—the area is pretty desolate except for Camp Hemlock," said Charlie.

"Camp Hemlock?" said Jane.

"It's a summer camp for rich kids. They have about two hundred acres on the lake. It's all fenced in. Chief Carlisle thought it would make the perfect HQ for Porter and Evansville to regroup," said Charlie.

"Sounds like an amazing place. What are the facilities like?" asked Sam.

"The camp has several lodges, about twenty cabins, flush toilets and outhouses, plus all the camping gear and food anyone could ever dream of. The kids who went there were definitely not roughing it, from what I could tell," said Charlie.

"Weren't kids staying there when all of this went down?" asked Jane.

"Yes and no. The camp was in the middle of their weekly turnover of campers. Some kids stay the entire camping season; others stay for a week or so at a time. When the chief went up there to scope it out, the camp's numbers were fairly low because of the turnover. Over the past two weeks, some of the parents have filtered in to either stay there with their kids or take them to another location. Things have settled down out there," said Charlie.

"Sounds like the perfect place to me. Isolated, on a lake—with outhouses. Those factors alone solve many of the problems people are facing right now," said Mark.

"Yep. It was a good plan on the chief's part," said Charlie. "Plus, for most of the kids stranded up there, we represent their only line of defense against what's going on around here."

"A sanctuary for kids," said Sam, looking around at his supplies. "Make sure you reload your ammo. I think we all almost shot through our entire load out back there."

"Pretty close to it," said Charlie.

"Yeah, it's the least we can do for all your help," said Jane. "When we figure out what we're doing, we'll have to find a way to get some of these supplies to HQ."

"Aren't you guys joining us at HQ? I don't like leaving you here in the middle of New Order territory," said Charlie.

Jane and Sam shared an uncomfortable glance. Jane knew Sam wanted to stay out of the fray, and with Lea needing a long period of rest and recovery, she tended to agree that it would be safer to keep to themselves for now. At the same time, she felt a strong need to help her colleagues push the New Order out of their towns.

She also wanted to get more information about the current situation in the rest of the country. No one seemed to know what had caused the power outage. Most people were too caught up in their own daily survival to worry about anything beyond their front doorstep. At the very least, Jane wanted to visit HQ to piece together the bigger picture. Knowing how long they could expect to be without power or federal help might determine their ultimate decision about where to go.

"We're not sure yet, but I would like to get to HQ to figure out what's going on outside of Evansville and Porter. From there, who knows where we'll go," said Jane, with a hopeful look toward Sam.

"At the very least, we should check it out. We have our own supplies and food, so our presence wouldn't pose a burden on their supplies," said Sam. "If we decide to stay, we could send some people back to gather everything in here. What's the supply situation at HQ like?"

"It's stable for now. The biggest advantage to the place is that there's plenty of water and shelter for everyone. Plus, the camp had loads of canned foods. They're rationing, but it's still very livable," said Charlie.

"I could help round out the food supply with my crossbow," offered Mark.

"I'm sure they would love that," said Charlie.

"Well, if we ultimately decide to head out of the area,

we'll donate a large amount of this to the effort," said Sam. "Not like we can drag it along."

For the first time since leaving the mountains, Jane allowed herself to feel hopeful. They'd rescued Lea and were safely tucked away in their hideout. Charlie's description of the HQ made Jane almost believe that things would begin to straighten out. Jane leaned into the cot and nestled her head near Lea. The sound of Lea's deep rhythmic breathing filled the space, lulling her to sleep.

— 54 —

Brown sat anxiously in the Porter Police Department's communications room. He desperately needed to warn Marta about the New Order's next move. Time was tight. The best time to go to her was shortly after midnight, when she communicated with the police, but things hadn't settled at the station. He didn't want to wait too much longer, or the stations on the receiving end of Marta's transmission might shut down for the night. She could transmit warnings all night and nobody would hear them. He glanced at his watch. Another thirty minutes and he would head out of the police station. That should give the crew time to settle in for the night after the exciting discovery.

When he and Cherry had returned from their patrol, Cherry gleefully reported their find to the Boss. As predicted, the Boss went crazy. Brown guessed the Boss didn't care about the loss of the men. He was more enraged by the fact that the cops had run an escape ring right under his nose. The Boss turned his murderous rage into an unproductive search of the entire town.

A few more citizens fell to random gunshots, bringing the New Order no closer to discovering the scope of the human-smuggling operation. All they knew at this point was that the trail started parallel to one of Porter's main roads at the edge of town, like Cherry suspected. The guy with the big gun safe had been the cops' first point of contact on the trail. There would be more houses along the trail. The Boss was sure of it.

The Boss had the men walk the trail north as far as daylight would allow, which was when they discovered that the pig's cabin was far too close to the trail to be a coincidence. The guy with the big gun safe had been the first stop on the way out of town. Of course, Brown already knew all of this. He'd put it together as soon as he discovered Marta's midnight transmission.

Once night fell and the search ended, Brown knew it was just a matter of time before the men reached other houses along the trail. He needed to warn the police to prepare for the New Order's invasion and safeguard the people on the trail. The Boss had ordered his men to kill anyone they found along the trail, civilian or police.

Glancing at his watch again, Brown decided to bump up the timeline for his visit to Marta's house. He had done it before around this time without incident, and it did sound a little quieter in the hallways. Taking one last glance over his shoulder into the dark station, Brown felt confident that he would be able to leave the station unnoticed.

"Where the fuck do you think you're going?" sneered Cherry, from inside the dark building.

Brown rambled off a quick excuse. "I need to take a shit. You want to watch?"

"The Boss said everyone needs to be ready to roll out of here before sunrise. He wants us up that trail and on the cops before they drink their first cup of coffee. You'd better make it quick or they'll be looking for your sorry ass, too," said Cherry.

"I can always take a dump inside the station," said Brown as he left the station.

"No, thanks," said Cherry before nodding toward the back door to the station.

Brown moved quickly, trying not to raise Cherry's suspicions. Cherry followed Brown to the back door, holding it open as he moved behind the dumpster to the designated "shit pile." *Fucking asshole—he's actually watching to make sure I go back to the pile?*

"You want to come over here and watch?" he yelled.

Cherry glanced around, looking slightly embarrassed. A few moments later, the door eased shut, his shadow disappearing. Brown couldn't wait to be done with these idiots. He squatted for several seconds, holding his breath from the stench, before dashing out of sight.

The trip to Marta's house would have to be faster than he had previously planned. As soon as he cleared the sightline of the station, Brown ran to Marta's house at a dead sprint. Experience with the route allowed him to run in the dark. He no longer had to think about the best way to get there without being seen. Knocking on her door, with urgency, Brown waited for Marta to let him in.

~ ~ ~

Marta sat in her dark living room, trying to pass the time. She intended to wait an hour past midnight to touch base with Doris. The two had become friends through their nightly talks. Although their talks were quick and cryptic, the sound of another woman's voice soothed Marta. Loneliness, fear and boredom were a lethal combination for her. She relied upon the nightly ritual of communicating as her rock of sanity.

A soft but insistent knocking on the front door startled Marta. She slowly approached the door, wary of opening it. If a New Order man decided to pay her a midnight visit, she really had no way to defend herself. The image in the peephole was too dark to ascertain the man's identity. Wringing her hands, Marta debated her options. It really didn't matter. If they wanted to get in badly enough, she couldn't stop them.

"Marta, it's me, Brown. Let me in. I know you're there."

Marta opened the door. "What are you doing here? Is everything alright?"

Brown pushed past her into her house and closed the door softly behind him.

"No. Everything is not all right. The New Order found the trail. I've been waiting to get to you all day. They hiked it north this afternoon, but didn't get much further than the cop's house on the outskirts of town. The Boss is sending a massive search party to hike the trail tomorrow, right before sunrise. The men have orders to kill everyone they come across. Everyone," Brown said breathlessly.

"Wait a minute? What trail?" asked Marta.

Marta didn't necessarily trust Brown. He said he wanted to help the cops, but he also received food, water and booze from the New Order. For someone who supposedly hated the New Order, Brown seemed awfully comfortable with them. She had no idea if he could actually be trusted, or if he merely played both sides to his advantage. In either case, she would not reveal the existence or location of the trail. Brown could be tricking her in order to discover more than they already knew.

"What do you mean what trail? You know exactly what I'm talking about. The trail the cops have been using to get out of town. The New Order found it," Brown said quickly.

"I wasn't told about a trail," said Marta, straining to conceal her panic.

"Bullshit. There is a trail, and it runs roughly along Parker Road, heading north. It's an old horse trail. I don't have time for this shit. I risked my life to get over here and warn you. You need to tell the cops to get out, or their blood is on your hands, not mine," said Brown. "I need to get back before they figure out I'm gone. Tensions are really high at the station."

Brown left without further comment, leaving a stunned Marta standing alone in her living room. He had correctly identified the location of the trail. There were numerous trails in the area, but none that ran due north, parallel to Parker Road.

Marta ran to the attic, her older bones taking two steps at a time. She needed to warn Doris, fast. They'd be at her place by mid-morning if they moved quickly enough. Poor Doris sat alone and defenseless in her house on the trail. Turning on the radio, Marta adjusted the dials to eliminate the static.

"Hello? Doris? You there?"

"Hello? Doris? Come in!" Marta could barely contain her panic.

In the heat of the moment, she'd completely forgotten to follow the right communications protocol.

"Doris! Come in, please?"

Marta panicked that Doris would not be on the radio tonight. *Maybe she went to bed early? Or other runners were there? Or maybe Brown lied and this is some sort of trap?* An ice-cold shiver ran through her. She put the radio down and lifted her hand to turn it off, feeling the sharp edges of panic prickling her body. *Were the New Order men listening? Did Brown trick her into using the radio? Shit!*

"Marta, it's Doris. Are you okay? Over," said Doris.

Marta paused, carefully choosing her words. If Brown's plea had been a trick and the New Order was listening to her broadcast, she was as good as dead—but she wasn't going to give away any information that might make Doris's situation worse.

"Doris, listen to me very carefully. You need to get out of your house immediately. They found the trail—you're not safe at the house."

"Holy—uh, I mean—copy that. How long do I have? It's after midnight. I can't leave in the pitch dark. What should I do?" said Doris, the pitch of her voice increasing.

"They will be running in your direction before first light, but they might be listening to this broadcast. You need to get out of there tonight," said Marta.

"Okay. I can do that. I think I know where to go," said Doris.

"Don't tell me where you're going," said Marta. "Just get out of there."

"I understand," said Doris, with a shaky voice. "Take care of yourself."

"Never mind me. I'll be fine," said Marta. "I'm signing off. Good luck."

Marta's hand trembled as she turned off the radio. She expected the door to her house to come crashing in at any moment. When several minutes passed in complete silence, she began to believe Brown. She still didn't trust him, but if this had been a setup, those animals would have kicked her door in by now. There was nothing to be gained by letting her live.

Her message had essentially shut down the trail and her lifeline to the outside world. The police wouldn't contact her again, based on her report to Doris. She'd done the right thing letting Doris know that the New Order might be listening, but it meant she was completely on her own. The only thing she could do at this point was hope that Brown told the truth. The alternative scenario terrified her. They would torture her for information she didn't have. Charlie had purposefully compartmentalized the information for everyone's safety. All she could do now was wait—and pray.

~ ~ ~

Brown sat across town, in the dark communications room, listening to Marta and Doris chatting about the New Order's discovery. His plan worked like a charm. Hopefully he'd earned enough goodwill with this act to buy himself a pardon when law and order returned to Porter and the surrounding areas.

— 55 —

Charlie heaved his overloaded backpack onto his shoulders and took another sip of water.

"You about ready, Mark?" asked Charlie.

"Whenever you are."

"We'll need to check the surrounding area before we open the door. You never know if anyone has joined us," said Sam.

"I wondered how you might do that," said Mark. "Be an awful surprise to find someone staring at you on the other side."

"Not being able to observe our surroundings is a huge disadvantage to the storage unit idea. I have a small wireless camera on one of the shelves that I can install at some point. Just need to figure out a way to discreetly wire and power the thing. I hadn't worked all that out yet," said Sam.

"What do we do in the meantime?" said Charlie.

"Hold on. I need to move the clamps," said Sam.

Sam moved the clamps about four inches up the track and then refastened them. Grabbing a small, telescoping inspection mirror that he had hung from one of the walls, Sam lay flat on the ground.

"Okay, lift it as slowly and quietly as possible until you reach the blocks," directed Sam.

Mark and Charlie eased the heavy metal door up a few inches until it reached the blocks and the door would not budge any further. Once the door stopped, Sam slid a small wooden brick under the edge of the door to keep it wedged open.

"You can let it go," whispered Sam.

The two men let go of the door, the wood brick holding it up.

"You really thought of everything," whispered Charlie.

"Thinking of survival scenarios has sort of taken over my free time," said Sam.

"Sort of?" said Jane.

"Guilty as charged."

Sam slid the mirror under the opened door and turned it to look down the entire length of the storage facility in both directions.

"How does it look?" asked Charlie, kneeling next to Sam.

"Like nothing changed from last night," said Sam, pulling the mirror inside. "Give me a second to remove the clamps so we can open the door."

Once the clamps were removed, Mark and Charlie rolled the door halfway open and stepped out into the cool morning air. Charlie took a deep breath of fresh air. It felt good to be outside.

"Be careful out there," said Sam.

"We'll see you in a few days at HQ. We need to give Lea some time to rest before we head out," said Jane.

"No problem. We'll be there. Are you sure you're good with the directions I gave you?" said Charlie.

"We should be fine. I have a rough idea where the

camp is, and your map will fill in the details," said Sam.

"Good luck, guys," said Mark.

"You too!" said Jane.

Charlie and Mark had reached the fence before they heard the storage locker door clink back into place. The metallic sound carried across the silent night far more than he would have expected. He had half a mind to go back and tell Sam. If anyone had been walking the fence line near the woods, they would have heard enough to pique their interest. Unfortunately, they didn't have the time to spare. They'd taken longer than anticipated at the locker, and he needed to get to Scott's house before Mike did anything rash.

Mark peeled back the chain-link fence, allowing Charlie to pass through. Once on the other side, they worked to get the fence back in place. A New Order truck passed in the distance. Fearing for the worst, Charlie wondered if the night would be longer than he originally anticipated. He thumbed the safety of his rifle back into the fire position and walked into the night.

~ ~ ~

Jane and Sam sat quietly next to each other on a thick wool blanket while Lea quietly dozed. Sam leaned into her, pulling her close to him. Jane felt good in Sam's arms. She loved these quiet moments together. Despite their situation, Jane felt safe and loved. They had their daughter, plenty of supplies and most importantly—each other. The rest would fall into place soon enough.

"What are you thinking about?" asked Sam.

"I'm thinking about how lucky we are that you did all of this," said Jane.

"To be honest, I never thought I'd hear you say that. At times I began to think maybe things were getting out of control. Kind of cringing whenever the bank statements arrived. Now I'm really glad I never stopped planning," said Sam.

"Me too. I figured you knew what you were doing, so I never raised an eyebrow," said Jane. "When do you think Lea will be ready to move?"

"In a day or so. She has been through a lot and just needs some time to rest."

"I have no problem with that. A few days in a storage locker never hurt anyone." Jane smiled.

"That's something I thought I'd never hear in my lifetime," said Sam. "Or want to hear."

They both laughed softly before Sam gently kissed the side of Jane's head.

— 56 —

Doris raced through her house, grabbing the last of the supplies she could fit in one of her son's old camping backpacks. The thought of the New Order thugs coming up the trailhead had galvanized her into action. Charlie had warned her that this day might come. Despite his repeated warnings, Doris had felt relatively safe at the homestead. Her place seemed too remote for the New Order men to find, and she'd never actually seen the men in action. The whole thing seemed like a dream to her. A far removed nightmare at worst. Now the whole mess was headed her way.

She'd briefly considered heading north on the trail immediately after Marta's warning, hoping to put as much distance between herself and the house as possible, but dismissed the idea after checking on the conditions.

Without the aid of a flashlight, she couldn't see the ground in front of her, and one wrong step in the dark with a heavy backpack could put a sudden end to her trip. Then what? Crawl off the trail and hope nobody discovered her path? And there was no way she could risk using a flashlight. She'd be an obvious target fumbling around with a flashlight in the dark. She was better off staying put for now and leaving at first light, when she'd still have a sizable head start on the New Order posse. Plus, she had plenty of things to take care of before she left.

Doris tried to hide as many things as she could. She stuffed the rafters in the barn with tools, gas cans and oil for the machinery. The root cellar became a secret hiding spot for jars of canned foods, dried foods and anything else from the kitchen she thought might be helpful later if she was able to return to the house. The root cellar's location was not obvious from the house, and she hoped they might not find it.

After spending a number of hours putting the house in order, she gathered up her son's items from the mantel and headed upstairs to her bedroom. The wooden planks in her closet lifted out of place to reveal a small, hidden nook beneath. Doris stuffed the nook with sentimental objects that she knew the New Order would likely destroy. Pictures of her son, his ribbons, burial flag and uniforms were neatly packed away for safekeeping. She had no intention of allowing the New Order to dishonor her son.

Taking one last look at her quiet bedroom, Doris went downstairs with a heavy heart. She knew that once she left the house, she might never come back. Once she finished these chores, Doris lifted the heavy pack onto her shoulders and took a last look at the beautiful farmhouse. The thin light-blue line peeking over the eastern tree line told her it was time to get moving.

On the front porch, Doris picked up the blue flowerpot, her signal to Charlie and any runners that the house was safe to enter. The flowerpot had represented a beacon of hope in a chaotic world. She threw it high into the center of the lawn, hearing it smash to pieces. Maybe hope was lost. Shaking the grim thought, Doris headed north to the edge of the clearing, taking her first steps toward the refuge that hopefully awaited her.

Continue the adventure with
RESIST AND EVADE
Book 2 in *The Blue Lives Apocalypse* series

Available at Amazon Books

264

Please consider leaving a review for Survive and Escape. Even a short, one-line review can make all of the difference.

Thank you!

For VIP access to exclusive sneak peeks at my upcoming work, new release updates and deeply discounted books, join my newsletter here:

eepurl.com/ctOGAD

About the Author

Lee West is the pen name for a well-known constitutional scholar and liberty advocate. Lee resides in the heart of "flyover" country, balancing a professional career with the joys of a hectic family life, two tireless dogs, and a community of friends. Lee particularly enjoys spending time outdoors with family, regardless of the weather! From snowshoeing to kayaking, cross-country skiing to hiking, mountain biking to recreational shooting, Lee brings (drags!) the entire crew along—even if the dogs are the only willing participants.

As a military veteran, Lee has spent countless hours advocating on behalf of veterans for increased benefits, better representation and more equitable treatment by employers and the government. Lee stands proud with the millions of veterans who have sacrificed in the past to preserve liberty at home and abroad—and all of those who carry that torch forward today.

Lee has also spent a significant amount of time working closely with the selfless professionals comprising our justice system—from law enforcement agencies to our courts. *The Blue Lives Apocalypse* series is dedicated to the "men and women in blue," who show up without fail or question.

Lee encourages you to reach out with questions about the series at leewestbooks@gmail.com.

Made in the USA
Las Vegas, NV
06 January 2022